Leaving Footprints

Leaving Footprints

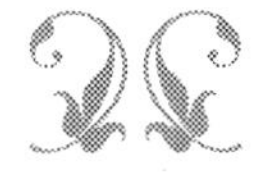

Tonya Painter

Order this book online at www.trafford.com
or email orders@trafford.com

Most Trafford titles are also available at major online book retailers.

Printed in the United States of America.

ISBN: 978-1-4669-1090-4 (sc)
ISBN: 978-1-4669-1091-1 (e)

Trafford rev. 02/03/2012

www.trafford.com

North America & International
toll-free: 1 888 232 4444 (USA & Canada)
phone: 250 383 6864 • fax: 812 355 4082

A NOTE TO THE READERS

Leaving Footprints is a work of fiction. Names of people dear to me have been used for entertainment purposes only. The character portrayed may, or may not, be based on relevance. Any resemblance to actual events or persons, living or dead, is coincidental. Although some real galleries, shops, businesses, and the like—are mentioned, all are loosely bound and used fictitiously within the story.

There is some truth behind factual evidence, but that is for you to discover on your own. Your adventure awaits. Which path will you choose?

This book is dedicated to my beautiful daughters,
Raechyl and Rebekah,
To my loving and patient husband,
Roy Wesley,
and to my best friend
who encouraged me to complete my story,
Jan Long.

Some people come into our lives
and leave footprints on our hearts
and we are never the same.

Some people come into our lives
and quickly go . . . Some stay for a while
and embrace our silent dreams.

Some people awaken us
to newer and deeper realizations . . .
for we gain insight
from the passing whisper of their wisdom.

Some people come into our lives
and they move our souls to sing
and make our spirits dance.

Some people come into our lives
and leave footprints on our hearts
and we are never ever the same.

—Flavia Weedn

One and two and three and four and five . . .
One and two and three and four and five . . .

I felt pressure on my chest as my lungs expanded with air. I could hear voices around me, but could not understand the words spoken. Muffled tones of urgency. I tried to move, but my arms and legs did not respond. I tried to speak, but no words left my mouth. "Someone call 911", a masculine voice cried out.

It is a typical summer day in our small town of Lewisburg. Children playing in the local water fountain downtown, tourists browsing through specialty stores, and old men sitting in barber chairs discussing politics. Excitement and crime are two things that rarely occur here. Our town is full of doctors, lawyers, and "old money". If there is a crime committed, these three factors keep it from making front page news.

"Rachel, can you hear me?"

I could hear this voice as clear as I'd heard it this morning asking me to drive my sister to school. A mother's voice is so distinctive. A mother's voice in distress sends chills down your spine. Why was she asking if I could hear her? Of course I could.

"Rachel, please! Don't you dare leave me!" I could hear the desperation in her voice pleading with me. Once again, I made efforts to move or talk. Nothing . . . What was wrong with me? I'm right here. With every part of my being, I concentrated on opening my eyes, moving my hands, and of course . . . breathing. The pressure on my chest was more intense. My body was numb as it contracted with the rhythmic movements of the voice above me. One and two and three and . . . .

"There's a pulse! She's back. Give us some room. Rachel, everything will be alright. Just relax. Help is on the way." With hearing this, I opened my eyes slightly. I could see my mother's silhouette hovering over me. Her eyes filled with tears and her face distorted in fear. I glanced around, but did not recognize the others that gathered around me, nor did I know where I was. I could only hear water trickling like a leaking faucet. The air smelled like my grandparent's damp, mildewed basement.

"Where am I?"

"You are at the Old Persinger Farm. We're not sure how you got here or why, but that's not important right now. We need to get you to the hospital to make sure that you didn't break anything from the fall." The fall? I could tell from my mother's tone that I was in serious trouble. I tried to remember what happened, but everything was blank. I don't recall traveling to the farm, nor do I have any idea why I would be there. It was an old, abandoned farm house located on the outer boundaries of town. What was once a beautiful, two-story white brick home was now three walls and crumbled blocks. There was no roof or second floor, just the remnants of a stone fireplace. As my eyes focused, I could see that I was actually under the house. It must be a cellar or some type of basement. There were a few broken stairs and the only visible light came from the flashlights of my rescuers. I conjured up the courage to ask the group how they found me. I had only heard the rumors about this place and none of them would give me a reason to be here. The only response I heard was that same male voice and he said, "Luck".

Luck. That was not a word that I routinely used. The only luck that I ever had was bad luck. There could be five life jackets on a sinking boat filled with six passengers and I would be the one dog paddling frantically to the shore. Luck. Freckles, fair skin, new city every two years, bratty younger sister, no friends, . . . that's my luck. My parents have been divorced for as long as I can remember. My father has been too busy chasing his dream to become the next Donald Trump that he doesn't have enough time to play the role of dad. My mother does the best she can raising two children on her own. The three of us live in a small home below the typical standards of Lewisburg. No gates, no paved circle drive, no pool. Just your basic, vinyl-sided home located within a subdivision. On one side, we have the Baker's. They are unusual to say the least. They are quiet and you never see them outside much, except when the older children are acting out their dungeon and dragons skits. Our other neighbor, Ms. Wade, is like our grandmother. She is an elderly woman that watches my sister when my mother works evening shifts at the shop. I pick her up after I get home from school, but I do enjoy visiting with her for a while. She tells the most unique stories about her childhood, over and over, and bakes cookies every evening. What else could a teenage girl want in life?

"Young lady, you have a lot of explaining to do! If it wasn't for Sarah you'd be dead. What were you two doing? No one ever comes here anymore. Haven't you heard the stories? Are you out of your mind?" On and on and on . . . . At this point all I heard was "Blah, blah, blah . . ." Although I started tuning her out, I did question one thing: Who is Sarah? I had no clue who my mother was talking about. I knew no one by that name. We moved to Lewisburg about one year ago and I haven't been able to make a lot of friends. It was difficult for me. I've really never had someone to call a true friend. When you move as much as we have, friends are not top priority. As I listened to my mother ramble on about this person by the name of "Sarah", I looked bewildered. I'm honestly thinking at this point that she has lost her mind.

"Sarah said that you two came here looking for something. Something for school. What could you possibly need for school from this place?" As I once again looked around, I could only imagine what she was thinking. There was nothing left but bricks and mud at this site. There was only one house within sight from this rubbish and the people that lived there were not kind to visitors. There were signs visible from the property line that clearly stated their feelings about unwelcome guests. I wouldn't dare take my chances on finding out if they would carry out their threats. This farm is definitely in the "backwoods".

She continued mumbling about my intentions and my friend, Sarah. But as many children do, I blocked out her words and started investigating my surroundings. I couldn't stand, but I was able to sit up against the better judgment of those around me. My curiosity has the best of me and I need to try to understand what brought me here.

"Where is Sarah?" I decided to ask my mom this question knowing that she would probably see it in my eyes that I was grasping for straws. I never have been able to fool my mother, but I knew that at this moment I would have to put my best acting skills in progress. If someone was concerned enough to help me and call me their friend, the least I could do is find out who it is.

"Rachel, I'm not sure. I got a phone call at the shop. The girl told me that it was an emergency, you two were here for a school project, you fell at the farm house, and to send help. She said she had to leave you to go call for help, but she would meet us here. She never came back."

I could hear the ambulance coming. It made a horrible crunching noise as the tires fell into the pot holes that formed in this mud pit called a road. It was easy to see that this area of Lewisburg did not receive the preferential treatment of the downtown, "rich" area. To be honest, I'm surprised that the ambulance even knew where to go. Unlike most public access roads, this area did not even have road signs. The best directions given would be to travel down the big hill, up the big hill, look for the row of baseball bat beaten mailboxes, and turn left on the muddy, gravel road.

Within minutes the ambulance crew had me on a board, lifting me into the air, and hooking me to a pulley like system raising my body to ground level. My senses are telling me that it is definitely evening. That must be the reason that the lighting was scarce and flashlights were our hope for visibility. They loaded my body into the ambulance and we were on our way to the hospital.

The ride to the hospital was the most excitement I'd had since moving to this area. Racing across town, the siren blaring, and a cute boy by my side. I would catch him glancing my way occasionally, probably wondering what would possess me to go to the abandoned farmhouse this late in the evening. That would be the question for the hour, not just for others but myself. Coming to a screeching halt, the boy unbuckled me and decided to start the upcoming interrogation that I would face the rest of the night.

"Can I ask you a question? I know it's none of my business and you don't have to tell me anything. Others judge before having all of the information, but I'm an open-minded guy and full of curiosity."

"Sure, knock yourself out. I don't think my day could get much worse."

"What were you thinking going to that farm?" The intensity in this young man's eyes made me feel somewhat apprehensive. I must admit that I had heard that there was some suspicious activity at the farm, but I didn't know the details. At this moment, I realized that I would now gain more information about the rumors than I would ever need.

"Look, I haven't lived here long. I have heard rumors, but that is what I take them for . . . rumors. I've learned not to believe everything you hear.

Every town has its stories." I looked to the rear door knowing it would open at any minute.

"I'm sorry. I didn't mean to offend you. My name is Colton, but everyone calls me Cole. I've seen you at school. Wait," he leans over to fix my oxygen tubing, "let me help you." He gently brushes hair behind my ears as he tightens the cord under my chin. I finally got a good look at the boy's face. I have seen him around school. He is one of the athletic jocks that I try to avoid at all costs. There have been times that I have walked hundreds of steps out of my way to avoid that crowd of rambunctious boys. Not that they've ever done anything to annoy me, but I'm smart enough to realize that I would never be a part of this crowd. Occasionally, I would witness several of them making sarcastic remarks about other students. Why would I subject myself to this torture? We'd be moving again soon enough so I would rather stay invisible. "Are you feeling okay? You look a little pale." His voice sounded genuinely concerned. Looking at his beautiful face, I felt weak in the knees. I wasn't sure if it was a direct result of the accident or if it was embarrassment mixed with a touch of infatuation. This Greek god before me with dark, tousled hair, chiseled jaw line, olive skin, muscular physique, . . .

"Yeah, I'm fine. I'm just feeling a little weak. It's all a little overwhelming." I knew that I had to say something fast or Cole would begin to understand my thoughts. At that moment, the door opened and there were two men waiting to rush me into the hospital. "Why am I at the hospital anyway?"

"You have a nice bump on your head. You were unconscious. It's all routine. Just let them check you out, run a few tests, maybe stay the night, and if you're on your best behavior you'll be out of jail by tomorrow." White, vibrant teeth peered through the plump lips of this angelic face. My heart raced as his eyes connected with mine. I had to look away.

"Well, Miss Rachel, here we are." With that being said, the crew lifted the stretcher and off we went into the Emergency room. I haven't had the pleasure of visiting the hospital, a large, tan brick building with immaculate landscaping. I've always been afraid of this type of environment and today would be no exception. "You need to relax." Cole rested his hand on my shoulder and flashed me that reassuring smile to let me know that I would be okay. He must be able to see the fear on my face.

"Where's my mother?"

"She's right behind us. She will need to fill out paperwork while we take you back. Don't worry, you are in good hands." For some unknown reason, I believed him. His voice was so reassuring. He must say these charming things to all of the high school girls. I guess that would help your chances on getting a date to prom or being crowned "Mr. Popularity".

The stretcher stopped behind a long, yellow set of curtains. I guess this would be my little room for the next several hours. There were several nurses that came in, all having various jobs. Each was completing their own given tasks like a colony of ants. It was complete, organized chaos, if that is possible.

I could see someone walking up to me out of the corner of my eye. I was so focused on the IV's being started in my arm that I did not waste any energy turning my head. It was probably my mother coming to cross-examine me again about the day's adventure.

"I found this beside you at the farm. I'll see you in school Monday." I quickly turned to see Cole standing by my side. He began to lean in to whisper in my ear. I could feel the heat of his breath against my neck as he spoke, "Our conversation is not over." Turning briskly, he disappeared behind the curtain. The scent of his cologne still lingered in the room. It smelled like an expensive brand, not your Stetson off the Kmart shelf. A smell I think I will be able to remember. I couldn't wait until our next meeting. On my lap laid a broken camera. The lens cracked and the film door was slightly damaged. Why did I take this thing with me?

Hoping that Cole could shed some light on the incident, the coming weekend would feel like an eternity. What if he ignored me at school? What if he does this with all of the unpopular girls? I would be the main character of a cruel joke. I'm not a gambler and I'm not ready to take that chance. I've never met a boy named Colton. He doesn't exist.

I hate Mondays. Of all the days of the week, why does it have to start with Mondays. It's too difficult for me to get myself together after having a few days off from the normal routine. Not that I have an unforgettable routine or anything. It consists of trying to pick out an outfit that will "fit in with the others", dropping my sister off at her school, racing to my parking spot at East so I wont have to walk a country mile, spending six hours listening to my teachers attempting to expand our knowledge on various subjects, driving home, watching my sister, homework, and going to bed. To anyone else, it would be quite forgettable. To others it would seem redundant, to me, it is my life.

"Come on, let's go. You're going to make me late." Siblings . . . . It is amazing how they can block out the world around them at the least opportune times. My younger sister, Bekah, is a fourth grader who has recently discovered her outer beauty and changing body. What used to take fifteen minutes to get ready and run out the door is now a thirty minute, clothes—slinging, hair—teasing, mirror—gawking experience. I probably had the same agenda, but it's not something that I would ever admit.

"Bekah, Come on! You've been in there for over twenty minutes. I have to leave now!"

"Okay, okay. Don't get your panties in a wad!" The bathroom door opened and out came this perfect little child. Every strand of hair in it's place, pearly white teeth gleaming, shirt neatly tucked into her designer jeans, and an attitude to match. My little sister definitely fits in to the Lewisburg lifestyle. She will only wear the best of everything. All of her clothes must say Aeropostle, Hollister, whatever is in style at the moment.

Me, I'm happy with sweatpants and a tee shirt. I do not have anyone to impress, nor do I try.

"That is so original. Did you get that from your Judy Blume novels?" I said sarcastically.

"No, it would actually be from my Dear Dumb Diary issues. You are so yesterday." Oh, Monday mornings. We were out the back door and on our way to school. I couldn't wait to drop off "Miss Personality". Not that I do not love my sister, but sometimes I wonder what it would be like to be an only child. Maybe it's because I've had to grow up quickly or maybe it's because I'm just, well, me.

Our house is only about ten minutes from Bekah's school. I believe that it would be easier for her to ride the school bus, but our mother is afraid that she would find some way to get into trouble. She would be the child making faces at passing cars or the one drawing hearts and butterflies on the faux leather seats. I'm honestly not sure if it's genetics, but we seem to gravitate towards trouble. Either we discover it, or it discovers us. No two ways about it.

"Okay, Bekah, remember to go to Mrs. Wade's after school. I'll pick you up from there as soon as I can. Mom is working late again." This was a discussion that she and I shared several times a week. Our mother had to work late hours to provide for us and I could understand the situation. It didn't make it easier on me though. My homework, her homework, dinner, showers, the list goes on and on. I was not only the big sister, but many times I became the mother. Growing up fast is not a choice at times, it is a necessity.

The traffic was chaotic, as usual, for this small town. Cars bumper to bumper trying to reach their destinations. The noxious smell of fumes from my car filled the interior at each stoplight. I've even tried to stifle the odor with air fresheners to no avail. To travel with me is like stopping in a gas station restroom. You have the comforting aroma of gasoline and vanilla. What a combination! There's a new one for the Walmart shelves.

"Yeah, yeah. Drop me off here. I don't want everyone to see me. You know that." Bekah has a complex about my mode of transportation. When did fourth graders decide that it wasn't cool to be seen in a ninety's model Fiero. This car was quite the ride of it's time. Red, with only a few rust spots, this was a gift from my mother's friend who owns a junk yard. It only needed a few repairs and he knew that I would need a car to be able to get around town. It's not perfect, but it was free. That's the best kind of gift.

"Right here! See you later." Slamming the door behind her, off she went running down the sidewalk, past the police officer on duty and up the stairs to the main building. I must keep repeating to myself . . . it has to be the hormones, it has to be hormones . . .

Waving to the officer, I turned down the one way street leading towards downtown. Lewisburg and it's traffic. Stopping at the stop lights every fifteen feet. Why this small town needs six stoplights within a one mile radius is something that I'll never understand. I guess it's nice for the businesses downtown because keeping the traffic flowing through this area would ensure that the clientele continues moving in this direction. It's just inconvenient for those of us who have to be in homeroom in fifteen minutes. It doesn't help that this year, Lewisburg was named "Coolest Small Town in America for 2011." Great, just more people to aggravate me. More traffic, more waiting, more shoppers in lines, the Lewisburg charm.

Driving by the windows, I admire the magnificent inventory of each shop. Realizing the fate of the lifestyle I have been dealt that's all I can do . . . admire. As I pass by my mom's coffee shop, I lower the passenger window to see who is working this morning and to enjoy the essence of freshly ground coffee beans. The scent reminds me of my grandmother. She would take me to the market on Saturday mornings when we lived with her in Florida after the divorce. I haven't understood why we had to move here so quickly. I was actually getting used to our surroundings and my time with Nana. On these morning excursions, she would let me hold the coffee bag as she ground the beans at the local grocery store.The sound of the beans crushing, the fragrance of fresh java, . . .

"Hey, Rachel!"

Quickly my memories of grandmother came to a halt as I heard the voice of an angel. Forgetting what I was doing, I slammed on my brakes. Where was this voice coming from? Realizing that the car behind me had only missed my bumper by a few inches, I thought it would be a good idea to start moving again. From the window I could hear that the driver had become enraged due to the graphic, hostile language exiting his vehicle. All I could do at this point is laugh. How lucky I was not to be involved in a car accident on a Monday morning. I would hate to explain this one to my mother. Yes, mother, I was driving down the road thinking about coffee beans when all of a sudden, a voice from nowhere yelled my name, the car behind me collided with my bumper, and all I did was laugh. That wouldn't sound too impressive . . . nor believable.

"Rachel!" the voice said again. I quickly looked in the direction of the person, but could not focus at the moment. My head was throbbing from the adrenaline pumping through my veins. Completely ignoring my curiosity, I kept my face forward and headed for school. I couldn't afford to be late again. I've already racked up three tardy slips this month because of my little sister and her morning routine. I don't know what is worse, trying to get my sister ready for school or the actual ride to school.

The other bad thing about this small town is the traffic pattern. Once you get to a certain point, the road splits into a one way traffic zone. It is exciting, though, because for several miles, you can feel like a race car driver, passing your opponents, accelerating through the turns, braking only when you see the local police parked behind trees picking off their prey like wild jungle animals. Luckily for me, I haven't been pulled over, yet. I guess when they see my priceless, extravagant set of wheels they are too overwhelmed by its beauty and prestige.

Pulling into the parking lot is always a humbling experience. The campus is huge, but student-friendly as far as the lay out. The students aren't allowed to park at the main entrance. This area is reserved for teachers and guests. Our lot is located beside the gymnasium. Every morning, the traffic is backed up while young drivers await their turn to drive to the "backyard". Car, after car, at least fifty every day. The city should charge an admission for this local car show. Nothing but the finest. Mercedes, Audi, Lexus to mention a few. Children of doctors, lawyers, the rich ones, they are my classmates. When I pull into my assigned spot and open the door, the horrible crunching sound of the door turns heads. The fumes, the erosion of metal, the scanty paint job, I am the person to envy.

Grabbing my backpack and purse, I start up the steps into the main building. This school is much larger than the others that I have attended in the past. Even though I may not fit into the crowd, I do enjoy the classes and the teachers. It is a magnificent, comfortable, learning environment. The meager class sizes give me the advantage over many students because of my cultural experiences at different schools. I have been a student at three high schools up to this point. I hope this is my last stop. I want the opportunity to make friends, get involved with clubs and sports, and find my niche in this world. Speaking of friends, I must have had a traumatic fall because I do not recall anyone named Sarah. My goal today and the upcoming weeks, was to find this friend and thank her for calling my mother.

"Rachel! Are you trying to kill yourself or something?"

The voice of my angel. I turned to see the face of my Greek Adonis. My knees again weak and my heart rate speeds out of control. My palms begin to sweat and my stomach tumbles. How could this boy have so much control over my emotions. Never before have I met someone that truly made me react this way, to this extent.

"Colton. You were the one yelling my name downtown. Do you know that I could have been killed in a car accident?"

"Yeah, traveling at the speed of five miles an hour and being rear-ended could have been fatal", he said with a smirk.

"Well, I could have had a heart attack, you know." Immediately I thought, why did I just say that? I'm smart enough to know that I would not suffer from any cardiac complications in a fender bender. I can not concentrate around him, his beauty. Just at that moment, BAM! I tripped over my own feet trying to climb the stairs and dropped everything. How embarrassing. Promptly, I bent over to gather my things, not realizing that he was preparing to do the same. Our heads collided into each other. As I glanced up holding my forehead, our eyes locked and he gave me a reassuring grin. His hand grasped mine from my face and gently replaced it with his own. His touch seemed to alleviate the throbbing pain. Our heads only inches apart, his eyes focused to mine, the smell of his cologne . . .

"Are you okay?" Colton whispered softly.

I couldn't speak. I was so captivated by his whole being that words could not leave my lips. I could only gaze at his radiance in awe. His hand moved from my forehead along my jaw line and rested under my chin. With his hands, he gently lifted and embraced my face between the palms of his hands.

"Rachel, are you okay?"

"Yeah, I'm fine. I'm sorry about that. I didn't know that . . ."

"You didn't expect me to be a gentleman and pick up your things for you. Right? Here, let me get them." All I could do was stand there; motionless. Great, another bump on my head, this boy probably thinks that I am an accident waiting to happen. I need to put a warning on my forehead for those around me. Maybe I would need to invest in a helmet.

"There that should be everything," Colton stands handing me my belongings, "Where's your first class? I want to make sure that my patient makes it there safe and sound. I have a reputation to uphold, you know."

Speaking of his reputation, what is he doing talking to me? I am a complete loser compared to the other girls at this school. I could seriously damage it.

"Thanks, but I'll be fine, really." I tried to be credible. Nothing would thrill me more than to have Cole spend a few moments with me. To walk me to class would be an honor, but I didn't want to appear helpless.

"I won't take "no" for an answer. I am walking with you," He firmly grasps my hand and completes with a light squeeze, "Where are we going?" Cole insisted.

"It's your tardy slip." I replied with attitude, "I'm going to English, Mrs. Moore's class."

"Perfect, I'm going in the same direction."

As we walked down the hall, neither of us said a word. I was too busy observing the faces of our classmates and their curious expressions. I must say, this was the most gratification I have felt in some time. It was as if the girls were envious of me and "my moment". Around each corner was a different person, with a startling look for us. Maybe I have a huge knot protruding from my forehead. Maybe my face is purple and swelling. Or maybe, just maybe, I'm walking down the hall with the most alluring boy I've ever met in my life.

"How did your pictures turn out? Is your camera broken?"

"My camera is definitely broken. The lens is crushed and the back won't shut properly. I took the film to have it developed, but the pictures were all black. I guess they were all exposed. A real bummer. I've enjoyed that camera ever since my father bought it for me as a Christmas gift. It wasn't the best in the world, but it had sentimental value."

"Why don't you get another one?"

"Long story. One day, maybe." Our lovely walk came to an end at the English room. I didn't want to bore him with details of our family living on a fixed budget. My mother's dream of owning a coffee shop had put a strain on our finances and we lived week to week on her income. I am proud of her, though, she is living her dream.

"Here you go. This is your stop. Try to be careful and not hurt yourself. Those desks can be a little dangerous. You can poke yourself in the eye with your pencil. Your book could catch on fire in the sunlight. You could . . . ."

"You are a real comedian. I get the point." My hand raises in the air to stop his sarcasm, "Thanks for the escort. See you around." With that, I turned to enter the room. Everyone was starring at me. I was not used to this much attention. I must say that I do not feel very comfortable.

"Hey, Rachel!" Colton exclaimed from the hallway.

I looked back to him in astonishment wondering what sarcastic comment he could come up with now. His face appeared sincere yet whimsical.

"About the tardy slip," he gave me a wink, "it's worth it." He whirled and walked away chuckling to himself.

Colton. Maybe I have met a boy named Colton.

The three o'clock bell rang as I raced out of biology class. I wanted to hurry outside to catch a glimpse of Colton before he left. At this point, I have no idea what I'm looking for. I've never seen where he parks or what he drives to school. Part of me imagines him in an SUV, something massive and powerful. A truck that screams "I am saturated with testosterone". Another part of me imagines Cole in a shiny sports car, something quick to accelerate and corners on a dime. An eye catcher that proclaims it is the "ultimate driving experience". What it all boils down to is that subconsciously, I've convinced myself that Cole and his group of friends were of no concern of mine so I never bothered paying attention. Today, though, I am filled with hope and a touch of infatuation, enough to make me take notice.

I didn't want to look obvious so I decided to sit on the rock wall facing the parking lot. Frantically I watch as cars drive by one at a time. Black Lexus, Red Audi, Silver BMW, Black Mercedes, Blue Tahoe, on and on. I strained my eyes investigating the interior of each car and truck that passed. No sign of Cole. What am I doing? I can't believe that I honestly thought this was a good idea. Even if I caught a glimpse of him, what was I going to do? Jump up and down, waving my arms, proclaiming my infatuation for him. Defeated; I scoot off the ledge onto the sidewalk. Feeling cool air against the back of my thigh, I'm terrified to look at the back of my pants. I must have torn them. How embarrassing. My car, parked solitary by the parking lot entrance, appeared to be a thousand miles away. The dullness of its exterior made it stand out among the crowd. I can only pray that Colton will not look at my bucket of bolts and flee before he gives us the opportunity to be friends. My thoughts quickly dissipate as a draft of air once again lightly touches the back of my leg. I shuffle towards my lonesome car. Luckily, everyone is gone. No one will witness this humiliating moment. If only there was a video camera. These situations have made people thousands of dollars. It's quite simple: Are you willing to make a complete fool of yourself on TV for money? I would have one thing to say, "show me the money".

"Rachel! Wait up!"

As I wheeled around hiding by backside, I heard the school doors slam shut as Cole came running towards me. My mind has gone into complete panic mode. Now, not only am I a stalker, but also a girl with her backside exposed to the world. I have no where to hide. My car is still hundreds of yards away. Fight or flight. At this point, I realize that I have no other option than to pretend like nothing has happened.

"Hey, how are you, Cole?"

"Great. What are you still doing here?"

"Oh, I was on my way out and realized that I forgot some things in my locker." Overwhelmed by fear and embarrassment, I tried to keep our conversation to a minimum. I couldn't take my eyes off of him. He must have gym as a final class. He looks like he just got out of the shower. His hair still damp and tousled. Standing several feet from him, I could smell the aroma of his cologne as his skin glistened in the afternoon sunlight. My mind started wandering . . . .

"Where are you going now?"

"I have to pick up my little sister. She'll be waiting for me at the neighbor's house."

"I didn't realize that you had a sister. How old is she?"

"She's ten. Her name is Rebekah, but we call her Bekah."

"Well, that's cool. I'm an only child. I always wondered what it would be like to have a sibling."

"Yeah, I've always wondered what it would be like to be an only child. We have something in common." We both chuckled at my attempt at humor.

"Well, tomorrow my friends and I are going to the Lost World if you want to join us. There's always room for one more. Besides, you need to get out and make friends." He flashed me that charming smile and I think for a brief moment I actually stopped breathing. Again.

"What is the Lost World?"

"Lost World is a local cave about five miles from here. My friend, Nathaniel, has been working there the past few summers, so he takes us in on private tours and we go to unexplored areas for fun. He likes mapping the new tunnels for the owners. If you're not into that sort of thing I understand, but you are officially invited."

"I'll have to talk to my mother to see what her schedule is like tomorrow. If she has to work late, I'm on kid duty." I tried not to seem too desperate. I would love to go into a dark, secluded place with Cole. I could see it now, the ground would be slippery, I would lose my footing, as I start to fall, Cole would embrace me to keep me from danger. He would look into my eyes, holding me close to his chest, one arm behind the small of my back, the other brushing the hair from my face, leaning in closer, the gaze now is directed to my parted lips waiting for the moment he would . . .

"Perfect!" He exclaimed, "I'll look for you in the morning. Be careful, I'm not on duty tonight." He sprinted towards the corner of the building, "See you later."

Yeah, it was perfect. As quickly as he interrupted my daydream, he left just the same. I scurried to my car in fear that he would notice my ripped jeans. As I opened the door, I could see a shiny, black BMW in the reflection of the glass. The engine seemed to purr as it started in my direction. Although the car's windows were tinted, I knew it was Colton.

Slowly, it pulled beside me, the windows lowering, and a voice saying, "black is my favorite color". Confused, I just stare at him and smile. I'm wondering why he would make a comment about the color of his car. It is a beautiful car, but he didn't need to convince me of anything. Quickly, I sit in my car and wonder how I will prepare my mother for this one. How would I convince her to let me go with a group of teenagers to the local cave. I've never expressed any interest in making friends or partaking in any outdoor activity, for that matter, so I can't imagine her actually agreeing to this adventure. But, I am willing to give it an honest try. Honest try, I should say, in my attempt to deceive her.

Sitting in the afternoon traffic, I used my time wisely trying to conjure up a strategy. I could tell her that we have a science group project due and participation is mandatory. I could tell her that I have decided to pursue a career dealing with the migration patterns of bats. If all else fails, I can tell her the truth, that I am infatuated with the boy from the ambulance crew and I would be willing to risk my life being bitten by a rabid bat to spend time with him.

One stoplight, two stoplights, three stoplights, four and under the bridge to our neighborhood. Hopefully, my obnoxious sister will be in a decent mood when I pick her up from Mrs. Wade's. Her disposition is entirely dependent on if all of her friends are still her friends and if the cafeteria served chicken nuggets for lunch. If both of these are pleasing to her, the world will still revolve. At least around Bekah.

As I pulled into our driveway, I glanced in the direction of Mrs. Wade's home. To my surprise, there appeared to be no movement inside. Usually, I would see Mrs. Wade rocking in her chair by the front window. She had one of those huge bay windows with a sitting cushion. Gabby, her gray cat, will sit there for hours soaking up sunbeams illuminating through the glass. The two of them, without a care in the world, delighting in each other's company, living a simple life. No cares. No worries. Just love.

The small, brick home appeared so much larger than our cracker box of a home. The landscaping always well manicured and the grass is always a vibrant green and of golf course quality. Every week, a team of lawn boys swoop in and create this masterpiece. It's such a shame that she has to live beside us. I am the yard girl at our house. My idea of mowing the lawn is trimming the grass as low as you can, even if dust flies. The shorter you cut it, the longer it will take to grow back. Brown patches of dry grass and muddy tire tracks. That's the beauty of our yard. You wouldn't have the fragrance of freshly cut grass lingering in the air on a cool summer's eve, but instead a cloud of dust hovering overhead and four inch grass blades flying.

Crossing over to her property, I quickly removed my shoes so that I could feel the soft carpet of grass beneath my feet. Plush, damp, perfect grass. Water droplets clinging to each blade after the sprinklers retire for the evening. My mind swiftly leaves the comfort of my toes and all of my attention is drawn to the aroma of freshly baked cookies as I approach the entrance. It must be chocolate chip. Mrs. Wade knows that's Bekah's favorite. It must have been a bad day at school. Chocolate chip cookies mean that there is a boy involved. A broken heart.

Knocking on the door, I called out, "Mrs. Wade? Bekah?"

"We're in here." a frail voice cried out. I walked down the long, narrow hallway filled with pictures of children, grand children, great-grand children, children of the children's children . . . . What a long hallway. I think she has a picture of everyone who lives in Lewisburg and the surrounding twenty counties. While observing these photos, I begin to question something. Why is it that in every picture taken, we are told to smile? Sometimes, you just aren't in the smiling mood. As I look around me, I am surrounded by people who look like they need to be on an Orbit commercial or a friend of the "smiling Bob" guy. They are so phony. Every single image caught on film is a moment in time with each person is saying "cheese" at a precise moment. How original. It makes me think of my Aunt Aleigh. She is a talented photographer. After her trips abroad, she always shares her adventurous memoirs.

Aleigh lives in North Carolina. She is an interior designer. When I look at her success, I wonder what happened to my mother. One is making a salary of at least one hundred thousand dollars a year and the other is lucky to make one hundred dollars a day. My mother, Lyn, owns the local coffee shop. She says that it is her "fun" job. Years ago, she worked in the medical field, but after several surgeries and misfortunes, she was not able to perform her duties and decided to leave. She said that if stress from the job did not kill her, her co-workers would because of her increasingly negative attitude toward the place.

My mother decided that we could learn to live without. The more money you make, the more you spend. I can see her point, but I would like to dispute the matter and gather my own evidence by experiencing wealth beyond belief.

"What are you guys doing?" The whole room was in complete disarray. There were boxes scattered everywhere and clothes lying on the bed.

"We were getting some things together for the neighborhood yard sale for the Orphanage. I don't wear these anymore, so I've decided to do away with them." Piles of polyester pants and moth ball scented frocks precisely folded on the comforter.

"That's right. That's tomorrow."

"Are you going to help or do you have plans?"

"Well, Mrs. Wade, I'm not sure. There is a class project due that requires me to go to a local cave for research." Okay, so I choose to pick the first response. Isn't that what you're taught when taking tests . . . always go with your first instinct. My gut was saying "school, school, school".

"That sounds interesting. What cave are you researching?" Mrs. Wade is such a good soul. Her whole demeanor is contagious. Her goodness, her generosity, her honesty . . .

"Well, there is this boy that I've met and he has invited me to go with a group of friends to the Lost World Caverns. We are going to map out new tunnels for the owners or something like that. I'm afraid mom wont let me go, because she doesn't really know any of the kids." I looked into Mrs. Wade's eyes waiting to see disapproval for my attempt at deception. Silence.

"Well, honey, that sounds like a fun project. I can talk to your mother and maybe help her understand the importance of class participation. I was a teacher once, you know." I realized at that moment, I need to add innocence and naivety to my earlier statement.

"Whatever!" a small voice resounded from under the bed.

"There's Miss Sunshine. I wondered where you were." I lower to my knees to lift the bedskirt to find my headache, "Come on. We need to get home so I can start supper. We're having soup and grilled cheese, your favorite."

"Yeah, about ten million grilled cheese's ago, besides I've eaten. Mrs. Wade made me chicken nuggets and chocolate chip cookies."

"Bad day, huh?" I reach for her hand, "C'mon. You can tell me about it on the way home." I flashed her a look to let her know that I was serious. Normally, I try to play along, but tonight, I needed time to get my game plan together and also my wardrobe. What do you wear in a cave? What should I bring with me? My flip flops wouldn't work so what do I wear? Sneakers? Boots? Do I need a heavy jacket? Bug spray? Compass? What if we get lost?

"I have had a horrible day. Kadie told everybody that I like this boy named Seth."

"Well, do you, Bekah?"

"Yeah, but she promised that she wouldn't say anything to anybody. She pinky promised!" Bekah exclaimed. "You never break a pinky promise. That will get you three years of bad luck."

"It will be okay. Come on, we have to go home." Helping princess to her feet and leading her towards the door, I continue, "Thanks, Ms. Wade, for everything. When I get home, I'll look through our closets and see what we can donate too."

"You're not getting in my closet!"

"No, princess, no one will touch your precious wardrobe." Quickly, I led her outside and across the lawn to our home. I needed to find something to wear tomorrow. One thing kept crossing my mind . . .

What if he regrets asking me and changes his mind?

Homework done. Dishes done. Laundry done. Convincing mom to let me go to the cave with kids from school . . . here it goes.

I heard the car door slam and footsteps leading to our side door from the kitchen. Eight o'clock and all is well. Bekah was asleep in her room. Now was my opportunity to convince my mother to let me go to the cave with Colton and his friends. It wouldn't be easy. She is a skeptical woman. Slowly the door opens and in walks my mother, Lyn. As she strolled through the doorframe, the scent of coffee lingers in the air around her.

"Hey, mom. How was your day?"

"Not bad. We are doing inventory this week, so it's a little hectic. How was school?"

"It was good. Bekah was taking her time as usual so I thought I was going to be late again."

"Yeah, I heard you guys this morning. Even though my door is shut, I can still hear my little angels." Mom flashes me her brilliant, reassuring smile. I knew this was my opportunity to explain everything about my morning. The episode in the car, the walk to my classroom, the invite to the cave. Now or never.

"Well, after I dropped her off, I was panicking about being late. I didn't get a ticket or anything, but something interesting did happen to me." As I glanced up, I could see that I had her full attention now. "When I was driving through town, I was daydreaming about grandma and almost got rear-ended. Nothing too serious, though. Don't worry."

"Rachel we've talked about that. You have to pay attention! I can't afford to pay any more on insurance. Much less if you get in an accident and we have to pay for the other person's injuries."

"I know. I know. I will do better. But, on a good note, I did get to meet the boy on the ambulance again." I paused briefly to allow a response.

"Wait one minute. Before you change the subject, you need to explain to me what happened with the grandma and rear-ended story."

"Well, I was daydreaming when someone yelled my name. I guess I slammed on the brakes and the person behind me reacted quickly, thank goodness. No big deal." She peered at me through the top of her glasses waiting for more information. "Then, when I got to school, I found out who was trying to get my attention."

"Let me guess, the young man at the hospital." The tone of sarcasm left her lips so fluently.

"Yeah. His name is Colton. He actually walked me to my first class today. Real nice boy."

"Not too hard on the eyes either."

"MOM! How embarrassing!"

"Well, it's the truth. He appears to be a well dressed child. Good upbringing it seems. What do you know about him?"

"Actually, not a lot. I know that he is one of the school "jocks" and he works with the ambulance crew sometimes. That's about it. Oh, and he drives an awesome car."

"Yeah, sounds like a good boy. Handsome, athletic, caring, and good wheels. Just what any teen age girl would want." We both chuckled.

We sat at the kitchen table in silence for a few minutes, but it seemed like eternity. When you're trying to conjure up the courage to ask your mother permission about something you know is against her beliefs . . . I need a miracle . . . I traced the wood grain of the table with my fingertips.

"I do have something to ask, Mom. There is a class project to be done in Science. Colton asked if I would be in his group." I changed my tone, "I would love to be in his group." I glanced up from the table waiting for the bomb to drop.

"Be in it then. Why are you asking me for my approval?"

Hesitantly, I continued, "The project takes place at a local cave. The Lost World. I'm afraid that you won't let me do this because of what happened at the farm and you don't know these kids."

"Boy, you know me better than I know myself, Rach. But, I must say that if it is something necessary for school, you are wrong thinking that I would disapprove. You know that good grades are mandatory. The only way you will ever make anything of yourself is to make the grades and go to college. Just remember, Rach, keep your feet on the ground."

"So, it's okay?" I looked at her with suspicion completely ignoring her last comment.

"As long as I know where you are, who you are with, what you are doing, and when you are coming home, I have no issues with it."

"Gee, mom, do you need to know what I'll be eating, when I'll be eating, which way I'll travel home, and what I'm wearing too?"

"Good thinking! Add those to my list." Laughing at her own humor, I knew that it would be okay. I knew that my mother was giving her stamp of approval for my adventure with Cole. "So, when does this event take place?"

"Tomorrow, after school. Do you have to work late?" I started fidgeting, "I did tell him that I would have to see if I needed to get Bekah or not."

"I can make arrangements. You do what you need to do. I think it will be a learning experience and an opportunity to meet people your age." Peering over the rim of her glasses, she adds, "Just please be careful."

"Thanks, mom. I will be careful." I jumped from my chair and kissed her on the forehead, "One of the guys in the group, Nathaniel, he actually works there in the summer, so he knows a lot about caves. It will be fun." My smile consumed my entire face. I knew this was true because it made me cheeks hurt. Only a little white lie. What's the harm with that?

"Oh, by the way, did you thank Sarah for me?" Lyn interjected.

"Thank Sarah? For what?" My little white lie was getting ready to turn into a huge white disaster!

"Thank her for calling me. Is she in your project group?"

"No, I forgot to thank her. I'll try to remember tomorrow." The smile ripped from my face as my eyes darted to the floor, "We have so many projects due and tests to take, I completely forgot. Sorry."

"And my other question." My mother did not give up easily, "Is she in the group too?"

"I'm not sure yet who all is in our group. I know of Colton and Nathaniel. Sarah must be in another class, but she could still join us at the cave." That was the best I could come up with on such a short notice. One thing with my mother, you have to be on your toes.

"Well, get lots of rest. Tomorrow will be a long day for you."

"Good night, mom. Thanks." I practically skipped to my room. I'm not sure if my feet even touched the ground. How would I be able to sleep? I had to get prepared for tomorrow. I had to get my outfit together. For practical reasons, I think I'll wear a pair of jeans, a long sleeve shirt, a light jacket, and tennis shoes. Not your typical outfit for a date, so it is my safe outfit with the friends look.

Laying in my bed, my mind began to imagine what the next day would have in store for me. Butterflies dance in my stomach. I closed my eyes to create images of Cole in my head. His intriguing looks, captivating smile, and brawny physique leave me speechless. I am in awe of his beauty. Tomorrow I am hoping to learn more about his inner beauty. Or is it just a rich boy charm? I grab my pajamas from the chest of drawers and start removing my jeans. As I set on the bed and pull them down over my knees, I feel my face flush as I realize that today I am wearing BLACK panties. At this moment, I realize that Cole's little comment wasn't about the color of his car, he must have seen through my ripped jeans when I was at my car. How embarrassing! I will have trouble sleeping tonight. I lose my count at two thousand, one hundred and several sheep . . .

BBBBBUUUUUUZZZZZZZZZ . . . . the alarm clock wakes me. My morning routine begins. Get dressed. Yell at Bekah. Brush my teeth. Yell at Bekah. Brush my hair. Yell at Bekah. Eat. Yell at Bekah. Drag Bekah out of the house. What a good morning it is. We are off to an excellent start.

Traffic was better this morning. It seemed to move smoother. There were no major delays. I am hoping that this means a few extra minutes in the hallway. Driving into the parking lot, I frantically look around to capture a glimpse of Cole's car. To my right, there it is in all of it's glory. Black, shiny, sleek, amazing . . . just like him. However, he was nowhere in sight.

Crushed, I slowly climbed the steps into the front entrance and through the doors. Although the outside of this building seems so much larger, the halls appear to be smaller in size compared to the others I've attended. Maybe it's because of the large, dark blue lockers that line the hallways. Or maybe it's the huge showcases of trophies and pictures of prized athletes and their teammates that create the walls in the lobby. Nevertheless, I decide to take a moment to observe the photographs. For months, I've had no reason to even stop. Today, I'm wanting to observe Cole and his athletic side. Varsity basketball, team captain and point guard, MVP for the year. Varsity Football, team captain and quarterback. Varsity baseball, team captain and pitcher. His face is everywhere! Not only is he a beautiful creature, but he is also apparently extremely gifted in the athletic division. What am I getting myself into? "Wow, Mr. Lewisburg" I mumbled to myself.

"Hey, you!" Whirling around, I turned to see Colton standing right behind me. Chills run down my spine and my heart skips a beat. My palms begin to sweat and my breathing stops for a brief moment. I have to remind myself to breath.

"Hey, Cole. How are you today?"

"I must say that I am better now. When did you get here?" he pivots to stop me in my path, "I've been looking for you."

Did I hear him correctly, he was looking for me?

"Oh, I just got here a few minutes ago. Long enough to walk in and become a member of your fan club. Is there anything that you don't do?"

"Yeah, golf. I've tried for years, but it's not happening. As far as my fan club, that's cute. You'd be my favorite." He stretched his arm out and I felt his hand grasp my shoulder with a slight squeeze. I cannot believe that he is actually touching me. I turn my head to look at his hand and then to look at his face. Quickly, he takes his hand away.

"Oh, I'm sorry. I didn't mean to offend you. I'll keep my hands to myself."

Panicking, afraid that he has taken me the wrong way, "No, you can touch me whenever you want. Really, I don't mind. I was just . . ." I paused because of the look on his face. One eyebrow raised and eyes as big as oranges. "Well, maybe that came out wrong. You could definitely take that the wrong way, huh?"

"Rachel, you really know how to make an impression. I'll ask for permission next time." His smile put my stomach at ease. The butterflies were wrestling with each other, I hate it when they can't get along. "Here, let me carry your books." He takes my backpack and slings it over his brawny cobra shaped physique, "Are you going to your locker?"

"Yes. It's right over there." I pointed in the direction towards the principal's office.

"Let me see if I can guess it," His face like that of a small child playing a new game, "Don't tell me which one it is. Just play along." To humor him, I agreed. We walked slowly along the row of lockers as his fingers brushed gently against the metal. One by one, the tension builds. Occasionally, he would turn to me, giving me a grin, watching my expression. "We're getting close." He was right.

We passed three more lockers. His facial expression changing from a smile to puzzled amusement. He turned towards the locker before us, leaned forward, smelling the vents on the front, and gave me a look of approval.

"May I?" Cole reached his hand out and gently lifted several stands of my hair and raised it to his face. I could hear him inhale, pause as if he was taking it all in, then exhale. "This is the one. Number 202. Am I right?"

"How did you do that?" I was in awe. Now, I realize that not only is he gorgeous and sincere, but also telepathic or possibly the offspring of a coon hound.

"Do what? Am I right?" He was so proud of himself. Is he always this brilliant?

"Yes, this IS my locker. How did you do that?" I gaze at him waiting for my response, "What's your secret, your super sniffer?"

"No, not really. I can smell your scent through the vent. You hang your coat on the back of the locker door." His fingers point to the vents, "Your hair smells like strawberries. If you get close enough, you can smell it from the locker."

"Really?" I walked to the large metal locker and stuck my nose to the vent. Nothing. I don't smell anything. Turning back to him, "I don't smell . . ." Cole's hand across his mouth trying not to laugh, I realize that I am, once again, the victim of his practical joke. "Seriously, how did you know?"

"I asked in the office this morning. I told the secretary I needed to return a book to you," snickering he tries to apologize, "I'm sorry, that was funny though." He bursts out laughing, "You actually smelled the vent."

"You're mean. I thought you were serious. I would believe anything." I thought briefly about what Colton said, "So, my hair doesn't smell like strawberries?" A frown came across my face. I'm trying to fight it, but I can't.

"I said I was sorry. That was a cruel joke." he makes an attempt of a frowny face, "Your hair? Your hair smells like . . ." I could feel his fingers mingling through strands of hair resting on my shoulder. Cole looked at his hand in my hair and then looked into my eyes. "May I come closer?"

Not able to speak, I gave him a slow nod, giving permission to proceed. His body against mine, I could feel the warmth of his breath against my neck as he exhaled. One hand in my hair and the other hand on my waist. Fingers intertwined in strands of hair. Again, I could hear his lungs inhale, pause, then slowly exhale. I patiently waited for a verdict while enjoying the moment. His body felt so strong against mine. I felt helpless. It was as if I was in some kind of deep trance.

"Such a sweetness. I'm not sure if strawberries could possibly smell so wonderful. Maybe I should taste you?" Leaning in with his eyes shut and mouth open, I quickly interrupted,

"What! Don't you dare!" Terrified, I pulled away from his embrace.

"Gotcha! Come on, put your books away." Hysterically laughing, I gathered my books and we walked to my first class. Everyone looked at us, bewildered. Who is this girl with Colton? That's what their facial expressions were saying.

"So, what did your mom say?" I had completely forgotten about the trip. With all of the excitement of Colton trying to take advantage of me, I didn't even remember the most important event taking place this afternoon.

"She actually said yes. I brought some clothes with me." I opened my bag to reveal my belongings, "I wasn't sure what I'd need."

"Great! You'll be fine. Nate and I will have everything we need to take into the cave." Cole gently touched my lips with his finger, "You just bring yourself, that beautiful smile, and get ready for an adventure. Do you want anyone else to go? If you have another friend, we'll make room."

If I had another friend. How can I explain to Cole that I only have him as a friend, if you can call it that at this point. I've never taken the time to get close to anyone or let anyone get close to me for that matter. I thought I told him this before, but maybe he forgot. "No, I don't know of anyone."

"Oh, that's right. You are the loner. It's okay. You'll get to meet my friends. They are a little odd at times, but I think you'll like them."

"I'm looking forward to it. I'm a little scared." I start to fumble my words, "I've never been in the ground or in a cave, with a boy, or anyone else for that matter."

"No, you just end up under houses. I bet there was a boy there, you just don't remember." Cole gives me his signature wink. "By the way, we need to have a discussion about that. Tonight." He gave me the look of a concerned parent as we approached my class and stopped in the doorway. I don't understand what the big deal is about the whole Persinger Farm thing. I guess I do need to talk with him tonight. Hopefully there will be a right time to bring it up.

"Fabulous. Thank you for my escort. I feel so safe and secure in your presence." I said jeeringly.

"When you're trying to hold the title of "Mr. Lewisburg" you do what you have to do. It is my responsibility to help others at all times and look good while doing it." Sarcasm filled the air. He opened the door for me and nodded his head as if to say "you may enter, madam."

"Oh, you heard that earlier?" I felt a knot in my throat. I didn't realize that I had said that loud enough for others to hear. How embarrassing. "I didn't mean anything bad by it. Just that you can do anything and you are so popular, chosen for captain of every team."

"Well, it's hard being perfect all of the time. Sometimes, I just want to say to people 'I don't want to be Mr. Lewisburg anymore. I want to be Colton the Great'." It was getting deep. I had to punch him in the stomach. Not hard enough to hurt him, just to get his attention. But, instead it got my attention. His abs were as hard as a rock. The look on my face must have me gave away. Again, Cole just gave me his reassuring smile and a wink.

"My Lord, I will see you after school then?" I bowed my head in a mocking gesture, "Where should I wait for you, Colton the Great?"

"Mere peasant. I will have a carriage waiting for you in front of the castle." Laughing as he turned, he quickly raced out of sight. I guess forgiveness for being tardy is not allowed even if you are royalty.

The school day seemed as if it would never end. All of my classes seemed to linger on relentlessly. All I wanted to do was race outside after the school bell rings and see my knight in shining armor. I must admit that I am somewhat apprehensive about the whole trip. First of all, I am an accident waiting to happen. I'm not sure if it's a case of two left feet or just a hand-eye coordination defect. That is my main concern, that I would make a complete fool of myself in front of this gorgeous creature that is flawless. Fifteen minutes. Next, what if I do or say something inappropriate? Would Colton see it as inexperience or stupidity? I admit that I know nothing about caves or the outdoors or even boys. I have to block this out. The more my mind wanders, the more I want to tuck my tail and go home. Ten minutes.

I notice peering through the school windows, two tiny birds jumping from limb to limb of a dogwood tree. Their bodies so fragile. No cares, no worries; only fascination with the world around them. They were not concerned about how they look or what others would think of them frolicking in the tree. Moreover, their only thoughts were of an immediate gratification for the moment. They were living in the moment. I needed to learn from these creatures. Five minutes.

Little birds, my new teachers. I watched them contently; their intriguing dance. Suddenly, my eyes are drawn to a black, shiny object parked at the front entrance of the school. It was Colton. He wasn't joking when he said he would be waiting for me. He opened his door and leaned into the back seat, moving things around. He then stepped out of the car and waltzed to the passenger seat. I couldn't see what he was doing but he was fumbling with something in the front seat. Was I ready for this? RRRIIIINNNGGG. The bell sounded throughout the room. This was it.

Quickly I gathered my things and headed to my locker. I try to convince myself that everything will be fine. I remember the birds, carefree and vigorous, as I cram all of my books into the slender locker. No homework for me to take home this weekend, I managed to complete it all during lunch. All I need is my bag of clothes, my purse, and my smile.

"Hey, Rachel. Are you ready to go, girl?" A tall boy, with sandy brown colored hair, said in passing. I recognize this boy but I don't know his name. The word that comes to mind, "HOT".

"Excuse me?" I asked ungracefully.

"Oh, I'm sorry. We haven't been formerly introduced. I'm Nate. Colton's friend." Nate extended his hand out to consummate our greeting. As I reached forward, he quickly drew back his hand and embraced me in a bear hug. Squeezing tightly and lifting me into the air, I tried to pry myself loose from his grip.

"Oh, I can't breathe."

Suddenly, my feet once again were on the ground and my breathing resumed.

Cheerfully I said, "Now that I can breathe, yes, I'm ready, I think. I'm not sure what I'm doing. I've never done anything like this in my life."

"Don't worry, you are in good hands, Chica. We'll take care of you." Nate picks up my bag and hands me my purse, "C'mon, Cole's waiting for you out front."

I carefully placed my purse under my arm and followed this boy named Nate outside. I'm not sure if it's hormones or if every boy in Lewisburg is just gorgeous, but this Nate character was quite the catch too. His build was a little larger than Colton's. The gym must be his second home from the looks of his masculine physique. His eyes were a piercing shade of blue. I couldn't take my eyes from his when he spoke. It was if they demanded my full attention.

Through the entrance doors and down the front steps, there awaiting me was my carriage and knight. Like a true gentleman, Cole came from his side of the car to open my door. I felt like I was in a dream. Never before has anyone ever opened my door or even offered to give me a ride in their car for that matter.

"Thank you", I whispered as I walked around the corner of the door and turned to enter the car.

"Are you ready to play with me in the dark?" Cole asked sarcastically.

Thud! With that comment, I lost my balance and hit the back of my head against the doorframe as I stumbled backwards. Cole managed to catch me before the damage worsened. His arms around my waist and his face inches from mine, he winked and commented "This is becoming a habit, you know."

"I am so sorry. You surprised me with all of this and then the comment about being in the dark . . . ."

"I was only joking. I was trying to lighten the moment. You look very tense. You need to loosen up," his hands placed gently around my waist, "You'll be fine. I'm always here to catch you when you fall." A grin emerged from the corners of his lips. He placed one of his hands on the back of head and gently started rubbing the knot that was beginning to form. His eyes never left mine. Comfort and anticipation filled my body. Every inch of my body was trembling from head to toe.

"May I?" he asked reaching out his hand for mine. I extended my hand to his as he helped me into my seat. His complete control over every situation fascinates me. I feel powerless. He gracefully walked around the back of the car like walking on water. I look over as he opens his door and cant help but smile. My charming prince.

"Here we go. Nate and the others will follow us there. I wanted you alone. It will give us a chance to get to know each other better. So, are you ready for the interrogation?" he paused briefly, "I need answers."

My only comment was that I need things too and he is the person to give them to me, "I'm ready for whatever you have to ask."

"I know that you moved here about a year ago. You haven't been able to make friends, nor do you make that your goal at every school. You have a little sister, Bekah. Your mother works late shifts. How am I doing?"

"So far, so good. By the way, my mother's name is Lyn and she owns the coffee shop downtown. Continue."

"You are insecure about yourself and I'm not sure why. You are absolutely captivating. It does concern me that you are going out of your way to get attention. Like going to the Persinger Farm."

"What! I'm not going out of my way for anything!" Well, except getting Cole's attention, but he doesn't need to know that, "I'm not sure why I was at the farm. I don't remember anything about that whole day."

"So, you didn't go to one of the most haunted areas of the town for a little attention?"

"Yes, I went there and threw myself into the cellar because I had heard that you were on the squad that night."

Laughing hysterically, Cole had no clever comeback. For once, I left him speechless. There was silence.

"So, how does Sarah fit into this story? How did you meet her?" he asked with genuine concern.

"I don't know anyone by that name. I'm not sure who it is. Do you know this Sarah?"

Silence.

"Cole, do you know Sarah?"

"Yeah. Well, no. It's difficult to explain. She's not a student at our school. She's . . ."

At that moment, Nate and the others raced by our car and I completely lost Cole's attention. He was now focused on regaining the lead passing his friends on this abandoned country road. I watched painfully as we entered each curve in the road. My car would have fallen apart two miles back. Even though we were traveling at a high rate of speed, I still felt protected against harm.

"Hold on." Colton downshifted and accelerated quickly in the turn. My head whipped from side to side as the car clung to the pavement and we sped past the other vehicles. They were no competition for his car. I'm not sure what is under the hood, but it is powerful! We slid sideways onto the gravel road which led to the cave entrance. Dust and gravel engulfed the cars behind us. We couldn't even see them at this point.

"Is this how you all always travel here? Race?" I asked Cole.

"Yeah. It's a game to us now. No one has ever beat me. I let them take the lead until the final turn, then I get them. It makes the time pass quicker." So much for our conversation. But I know boys will be boys. Testosterone is contagious when you are of the male species. The biggest and fastest will survive and be crowned winner. Or Mr. Lewisburg in this case.

"Here we are. This is the Lost World."

Before us stood a large, wooden building constructed in front of an enormous mountain. I might be a little naive at times, but I do not see a cave. I examine the mountain side looking for a crevice or opening . . . nothing.

"Is this a joke? I don't see an entrance. Where is this cave?"

"We have to go inside the building. The entrance is inside."

Colton was so matter of fact that I had no reason to doubt him, but part of me did. All I knew at this point was that this boy's name was Colton and his friends were behind us. How trustworthy is this guy? Am I the brunt of a bad joke? Why here? There didn't appear to be anyone inside the building.

Our car came to an abrupt stop in front of the building. Nate pulled in beside us in his Jeep. It seemed to match his playful personality bright red, lifted in the air, big tires, and topless. The other car pulled in quickly beside Nate. After several minutes a boy and girl stepped out. Thank goodness another girl. From Nate's jeep emerges another boy. I guess at any moment, we'll start into a Mickey Mouse roll call session to acquaint everyone. Hopefully. Right now, I am feeling completely out of my comfort zone.

"You got the key, Nate?" The tall, black haired boy from the second car asked.

"Yeah, man, just carry your stuff up to the door."

"Stuff? What stuff is he talking about, Cole? Was I supposed to bring something?"

"You're fine. We always pack a few things, just in case."

"A few things like what? Can I ask?" There was an uncomfortable silence. Is it from Cole trying to find a nice way to tell me something horrible or is it . . .

"We never know when we might encounter a few vampires, blood sucking bats, or zombies. We have to come prepared with wooden stakes, holy water, and some crucifixes." With this come back, it was Cole's way of putting his humor into the right words. His wit fascinates me.

"Cute, you're funny." I punched him in the stomach.

"No, really, we always bring the map that Nate uses to explore, a compass, bottled water, a first aid kit, and bug repellant."

"Sounds like you all have mastered this caving thing."

"We're here all the time. You'll be so surprised as to what's under the ground here in Lewisburg."

I didn't respond to his last comment. My facial expression must have said it all . . . entirely confused.

"C'mon. You need to meet everyone." He grabbed my hand and lead me over to the others. It took me a moment to realize that Cole had my hand in his. This was too good to be true. If this is a dream, don't wake me up. The group had formed by the entrance door.

"Hey, guys and girl, I want you to meet Rachel. She's a new girl at school and I thought it would be good for her to come out and meet some good people." Immediately, my heart sank to my feet. Now, I realized that this whole scenario wasn't because Cole liked me, but he felt sorry for me. Poor little Rachel.

Not wanting it to look more than it was, I dropped my hand from his. He turned abruptly to look at my face to see the reason for my actions. I just raised my hand to my eye pretending that something must be in it.

"Hey, Rachel, I'm Nate. I'm the stud in the group. If you want to look cool, drop this jerk and hang out with me." Comedian Nate knows how to impress a girl with his flattery. Cole walked over and put him in a head lock followed by the "nugi". I smiled at Nate to show my appreciation for his efforts.

"Let me do it this way. This is a group of clowns. Down the row," Cole points to each as he introduces us, "this is Brandon, Lindsey, Tyler, and of course, you've met Nate." All of them smiled and said their hellos.

"Hey. It's nice to meet all of you. I hope I'm not too much of a problem."

Brandon smiled and said, "You're no problem. If we have to we'll leave you in there." Everyone chuckled at his response. I didn't know to laugh or to be scared. Colton came back to my side and put his arm around me. Even better, he gave my shoulder a gentle squeeze to reassure me that everything would be okay.

"Enough of this mushy crap, let's go! Everyone keep up." Commander Nate had spoken and the troops followed behind him.

Cole and Brandon walked ahead with Nate, Lindsey close behind, while Tyler was by my side. Tyler is the tall, black haired boy who is the definition of tall, dark, and handsome. His skin is a luscious olive tone and looks as soft as silk. Dark brown eyes and physically majestic. Even though we are on an adventure hike, he still manages to don preppy, golfer-looking attire. I cannot find any words to start a conversation, so I just say the first thing that enters my mind.

"So, are you and Lindsey a couple?" Lame. Why did I say that?

"Lindsey? No, she's my sister."

"I'm sorry. It's really none of my business."

"No, that's cool. You have to start a conversation somehow." he answered contently.

We took a few steps not saying a word. Entering the building my eyes were drawn to a gigantic, metal tunnel that formed one side of the wall. A pad-locked door holding the mystery of the cave inside. Nate fumbles with the lock until we all hear an audible click.

"We're in. Let's go." Nate called out to the group. One by one we all passed through the doorway and into the passage. It reminds me of going into the New York subway. The long stairway and the metal. Or, I should say, what I've seen in the movies. I've never visited the big city. Mildew and dirt are the smells that linger in the air. It brings back memories of the farm incident. How can two places so far apart smell the same?

"So, Rachel. You and Cole. What's the scoop?" Tyler asked.

"I don't think there is a scoop. He and I are just, well, friends I guess you could say." I wasn't sure how to respond to that comment. I didn't think of Cole as a boyfriend. Most importantly, I believe those feelings are mutual.

"No? It looks like more to me. Cole doesn't just take up with anyone, you know. He's rather picky. About his girls anyway."

"Really? I don't know enough about him to know that. So, what else should I know?" I put the bait out there, now I need to see if Tyler will take the hook. My knowledge about Colton is minimal and this is one person who could enlighten me.

"Colton Jacob Lewis. Let me see what I can tell you. His family was one of the first to the area, hence, Lewisburg. His father is one of the local lawyers and his mother is a doctor at the hospital. He is an only child. Spoiled, rich kid, but has a heart of gold. How am I doing so far?"

He was doing better than I could imagine. I didn't even know Cole's last name.

"So far, so good, but I knew those things. What else do you have?" I pretended to be closer to him than I really am at this point.

"He runs with the ambulance squad on certain days to help his college application look better. He is wanting to follow in his mother's footsteps. He has a 4.0 in all courses. He could go to any college."

"Okay, he is a genius. That's evident. What about girls? Has he had a lot of girlfriends?" At this point, I realized that the direct approach would work best for my friend, Tyler.

"Oh, girls. Well, actually, no, he hasn't had a lot of girlfriends. It's an odd situation. Rumor is that he hasn't found anyone suitable for his parents and family. Most girls are even afraid to approach him. His family demands only the best. I can only remember one girl. Her name was Tiffany. She lived here for about a year. They were really close, she met the family's requirements, but her father was transferred and she moved away. He was heartbroken. That's about it." Tyler's perception of the situation left me with a dismal feeling. Quite overwhelmed.

"How sad. To have found love and lost it. I can only imagine." My face looked to the concrete in front of me. I was crushed. Why did I ever let myself believe that Cole could like me? These past few days have been a dream come true.

"Enough of that crap, let's catch up to the others and get exploring." Tyler nudged my shoulder and gave me a huge grin.

He is right. I'm here to try new things and meet young people my age. I need to keep my feet on the ground and head out of the clouds. The others were far ahead of us at this point. I didn't realize how far behind we had drifted while consumed in our conversation. We quickened our pace to catch the group.

"It's about time you two joined us. Were you sharing deep dark secrets?" Cole questioned.

"No, man. I was just trying to find out more about your new girlfriend." Tyler has a way of just throwing that out there. I closed my eyes waiting for his response. My fear is that Cole will become upset and bringing me was the worst idea in the world.

"She's awesome, isn't she?" Colton looked in my direction and winked. "Come up here with me, baby, so I can keep an eye on you. We will be getting into the cave entrance in a few moments."

Inarticulate. I could not believe the words that I just heard. He did not deny the accusation of being his new girlfriend. I scurried to his side so that I would not disappoint him. With my eyes focused forward to the next section ahead, I did not notice Cole's outstretched hand until he cleared his throat, intentionally, to get my attention.

"Oh, I'm sorry. I didn't realize that your hand was there."

"I was going to give you two more seconds then I was going to pick you up and throw you over my shoulder. You can either come willingly or by force. Your choice."

"I'll pick willingly. I don't want to offend any of your friends." I innocently smiled at Colton to let him know that he was in complete control of the situation and I was going to follow his lead.

"Good choice. Now, seriously, are you ready to be with me in a dark, secluded place? One way out? No where to run? You are at my mercy." Colton's antagonizing humor still fascinates me.

"Lead on, Mr. Lewisburg." One eyebrow raised and pursed lips showed him that I meant business. Two could play this game and I was calling his bluff.

The mouth of the cave is larger than I imagined. I pictured this tiny crevice, one that you would have to get on your hands and knees or slither on your stomach. The end of this concrete passage opened into the mouth of the cavern. The sides a dull, grayish brown and jagged in texture. The temperature was brisk and cool. Nate was rambling on to me about how the cave stays the same temperature year around. This made me think that maybe my family should move in here. Who needs air conditioning?

"Look at that Rach." Cole is pointing towards a large, pedestal-like formation of rock extending upward from the surface of the floor.

"What is that?" I asked inquisitively.

"That is a stalagmite. In caves you have stalagmites and stalactites. One forms from the ceiling and the other from the Earth's floor. It is a work in progress. It takes years for these to reach completion. Nature at it's best." Cole instructed.

"It's beautiful. I love how it glistens in the light's reflection."

All of us wandered throughout this main corridor. I could tell that the others were starting to become a little bored as I inspected the walls of the chamber. I was in awe of the complexity of this underground world. There were several side tunnels and passageways. Each emerging into a different room, like a piece of the puzzle.

"Okay, gang. Today we will explore area twenty six. We left off there last week. We will be walking along the rock shelf by the underground stream. Everyone needs to be careful and watch your footing. Stay close to each other." Nate spoke in a direct manner. At this point, all jokes aside, he meant serious business.

I turned around to catch a glimpse of the overhead lights fading behind us as we descend deeper into the cavern. Our eyes were as good as the flashlights we held tightly in our hands.

"Cole, there is an underground stream in here?" I shined my flashlight from side to side looking for any trace of it.

"Yes, but we are not quite there, yet. It's really neat. The stream actually runs under the entire downtown area of Lewisburg. If you stand at the corner by the True Value store you can hear it through the water drainage run off in the middle of the street. There's some tunnels under there too."

"What? I've never heard that before."

"What the stream or the tunnels?"

"Neither. Does everyone in Lewisburg know about this stream? How can anyone build a city on top of a stream? The tunnels. Where are they?" I am utterly amazed.

"Many people know about the stream, but few know the complexity of the tunnels that lie beneath the roads and homes. You will learn so much in this little adventure. Just remember that what happens in the cave, stays in the cave. It's confidential. This is like area 51 and the aliens. If we think you will talk, we'll have to silence you."

"I'm really worried about that, Cole. Your idle threats are seemingly harmless. You don't have to worry." I shake my head and place my hand on his chest, "The group's secrets are safe with me. I do things and cannot remember. Did you forget?"

"Yeah, what was I thinking? You are harmless. Stop right here a minute." Cole put his palm out motioning for me to stop. I felt his hand gently follow along my elbow until his fingers grasped around mine. The warmth of his skin sent a tingling sensation through my fingertips. I froze in my footsteps as he released his grip. "Be very still. Don't move or say a word, okay?"

I nodded my head following his directions. I carefully watched as he slowly climbed into a narrow crevice on the side of the sloping basin. With grace and precision he lifted himself up and into the darkened area. All at once, I saw a hand emerge with an open palm. I knew what this meant. It was now my turn to ascend the ledge. I tightly gripped his hand and placed my feet against the wall, just as Cole had done moments before. My shoes slid against the wall as I struggled my way to the top. So much for poise. I landed abruptly tumbling on top of his tight chest. The radiance from the flashlight, resembling that of a candle, lit the small nook enough to see where I had landed. I lay there motionless as my breathing became one with his. My mind is telling me to move from him because he is probably crushing beneath me, but my heart is telling me that this is my chance to look deep into his eyes and let him know how attracted I am to him.

I chose to follow my heart. Colton chose to follow my mind. In a sweeping motion with one arm under my lower back, he rolled me over. I was now looking at him, our faces inches apart. His other hand, now touching my face, brushed along my cheek and then to my chin. The look in his eyes so passionate and full of desire. I could not look away. From my eyes and then to my parted lips was the path of his attention. He lightly traced the contour of my bottom lip with an extended finger. I couldn't help but bite my lip after he pulled away. My lip was quivering from excitement.

"You are beautiful" Cole whispered softly. His fingers entangled in my hair as he sweeps it from my face. He smiled and gave a quick wink. I knew the moment had once again vanished. I couldn't say anything . . . again. I just looked at him with delight as he continued to speak, "I wanted to show you the natural habitat of the common bat found in these caves. There is one little fellow that lives in this crevice. But when you threw yourself on me, well, I had to savor the moment while it lasted. Sorry about that."

"There is no need to apologize. I must say that I was enjoying it too." Stupid bat. That's what I'm thinking. Stupid, little, common bat. How much more will it take for this boy to realize how much I like him, so that he will let me have that one kiss. One simple kiss.

"Here, let me help you up. You have to stay in a lowered position. The ceiling is rather low. You start in first, okay."

"Okay. How far do I go in?"

"Just a couple of steps. Stay low and don't go too fast. Be careful. I'm right behind you."

The dirt floor crunched beneath my feet as we moved forward. Little pebbles made it difficult to keep stable footing. I found it difficult to maneuver into this area stooped over, but I was following specific orders.

"Rachel, stop. Right there, see him?"

To my surprise, at head level, there was a tiny, delicate black object clinging to the wall of this rock ledge. I looked at it's features for several minutes before realizing that Cole was using this opportunity to check out my backside. His eyes focused on my buttocks.

"Busted. You are so busted. Is that why you brought me up here to look at this bat?" Acting like I was embarrassed by his boyish ways, I whirled around to playfully confront him.

"Alright, so I planned on you falling on top of me, teasing you by touching your face, and hoping that there would be a bat in here so I could admire your beauty. What's your point?" Cole was now practically rolling on the ground in laughter.

"You should be ashamed of yourself. Luring me up here, teasing me that way, shame on you!"

"All in good fun. Come on, let's get back to the others. They are probably wondering where we are. We don't want a search party out looking for us, right?"

"What am I supposed to say to them if they ask me what we were doing?"

"Just tell them the truth. I tried to get you in a corner to give you a romantic kiss and chickened out. Or something along that line."

"Cole, how about I use the real truth, you were pulling another prank at my expense. I've become the main character in all of your comedy acts, haven't I?"

"That's not true. I enjoy spending time with you. I enjoy you. Honestly, my explanation is the truth. I did want to kiss you, but I didn't want our first kiss to be in a dirty, damp, smelly cave."

Wow. My heart is now beating so fast that I could hyperventilate. Colton Lewis just told me that he wanted to kiss me. Colton Lewis just admitted that he enjoyed spending time with me.

"Let me slide back down first and then I'll help you, okay?"

"What is this, another attempt to look at my butt?"

"You got me again. Will you please pay attention."

Cole slid down the wall on his stomach and when he reached the bottom, he extended his arms up to me. We could hear the others coming closer. Their conversations more audible by the moment.

"Okay, princess. Today."

I turned and grasped the edge of the ledge with my fingertips. The ground was damp and cool. I did not question his request, I followed my direct orders and lowered myself. Fortunately, Cole was there to support me as my feet slid down the side and my hands were frantically trying to catch hold of anything to find stability. Standing behind me, with his arms securely around my waist, he awarded my efforts with a modest hug.

"Hey, hey, hey. Enough of that you two. Will you come on!" Brandon exclaimed. We couldn't help but smile. Brandon's ball cap flipped backwards and his finger pointing in our direction reprimanding us like children. The rest of the group all smiling and laughing at our lecturer, Mr. Brandon McClung. He's your typical jock-looking boy. Tightly shaved brown hair, big blue eyes, always wearing a ball cap, brawny, and athletic. With one exception, he has both ears pierced with diamonds in each. He reminds me of that skateboarder named Sheckler. There is definitely a resemblance.

We didn't reply. Cheerfully, we once again followed, but this time, we were moved to the center of the pack to hinder another detour. We continued descending deeper into the cavern until we reached an area that Nate referred to as chamber G. Apparently, his personal mapping system is alphabetically arranged and extremely detailed. To the right of this section stood a mammoth stalagmite, pearl white in color. It bears the resemblance of a melting candle. Wax building up over time, day after day, forming an immense mound of polished resin. To the left of us, was a narrow, low ceilinged side passage that appeared to be unexplored. This primitive passageway, not accessible to the general public due to it's unsafe conditions, is abundant with natural debris and jagged, sharp-pointed sedimentary. Nate studies his map and immediately looks to the left. The story of the road less traveled comes to mind. Being that I am not one to take chances, I choose the road that has been traveled, every day by common people seeking a unique, no prior caving experience.

"Today, we venture into G1. Everybody check your flashlights. Let's go." With that, Nate maneuvers the group in the road to the left.

"Cole, are you sure I'm ready for this?" I whispered softly.

"You'll be fine. Just stay close to me. I am here to protect you. Enjoy yourself. Enjoy this opportunity to be with friends and see things that others will never see." Cole grabbed my hand. "Come on, Sunshine."

Carefully, I followed behind him watching every step he took. He is much taller than I so at times it was difficult to use the same foot placements. Slowly, we moved along this confined, moist, burrow. Maneuvering through tiny crevices, over boulders, and under hundreds of feet of earth above us.

"Everyone listening?" Nate asked.

"All ears." Brandon replied.

"We are approaching the area where in 1967 a prehistoric cave bear was unearthed. This section is difficult and it will require flexibility and strength, but it will be worth every minute of your efforts." Nate was glowing at this point. He is so confident and passionate about what he is doing today. He is definitely in his element.

"A bear? There are bears in here? Cole, you didn't say anything about bears. You only said vampires, bats, and zombies."

The whole group overheard me and started laughing.

"Don't worry, Rachel, there isn't anything in here that can hurt you, other than Cole. You need to watch out for him not the others." Tyler was joking, yet I sensed some sincerity in his comment.

"Thanks, Tyler. Glad you've got my back." Cole said amusingly.

"Seriously, guys. All joking aside, we are going into the cave further today to section G2. Last week I found an article about a "Bat Boy" that was supposedly discovered in this cave. The story says that a little boy was left in here and became part of a bat family. Rumors? Probably. Interesting? Sure. It's one of the only areas that we haven't ventured into from this location. Everyone game?"

"We're in, lead on, captain." Brandon called from the back. I thought he was in the front with Nate. How did he get back there so fast. With him is Tyler and Lindsey. I've noticed that Lindsey doesn't have a lot to say. She is a beautiful girl. Long, flowing blond hair, angelic face, absolutely Barbie doll material.

"So, what's up with Lindsey? She's very quite." I asked Colton.

"Don't let her fool you. She is not normally this way unless she is around Brandon. Nothing has ever been mentioned, but I think someone has a little crush on him."

"Well, that makes sense. I can sympathize with her." I say to him, but inside, I honestly believe that she has feelings for Cole. I can see it in her eyes.

"Look, here is the area that the bear was found. See over there. Come with me, I'll take you in for a closer look." I realize at this moment that Cole completely ignored my last comment because he was focused on the expedition. We walked through a gentle sloping tunnel off from our path. While the others jotted notes in their journals,Cole led me to the cave bear's final resting ground. It absolutely fascinated me. To be standing in the same spot where centuries ago, a bear took his last breath and this became his tomb. At that moment, I was overcome by sadness, feeling as if I was invading it's territory. I stood there in silence trying to imagine what life would be like in this surrounding. Not pretty.

"Are you okay, Rachel?"

"Yeah. I was just thinking about that poor, little bear. How horrible it must have been for him."

"It wasn't a teddy bear, girl. You are so cute." Cole pats the back of my head, "We'll come back later so you can mourn the death of Pendleton the Bear." Giving me his signature wink and putting his arm around my lower back, off we went to reunite with his friends.

I can tell that this next section would be seriously dangerous for all of us. Nate, himself had not explored it before. He is frantically checking the gear in his backpack. Talking to himself, nodding his head, he must be mentally checking off things that he needs. He removes his notebook from the bag and starts writing.

"What is he doing?"

"Nate? He documents everything. Time. Location. Explorers. He even draws a detailed map for future reference. Talent. That's all I can say."

"Does he get paid for these little side adventures?"

"No, not really. I think he is hoping to unearth something for the National Geographic. It's a desire to find the unknown. Like this "Bat Boy". Will we find him? No. Does it excite Nate? Absolutely. It's the thrill of the unknown. It's all about the challenge."

"Determined is the word that comes to my mind."

"Right. When Nate wants something, he will not stop until he wins."

For several minutes I sit admiring Nate. On the exterior he seems to be a huge prankster, but there is so much more to him. His intelligence captivates me. For him to know so much about something, to have such a passion for knowledge. There is more to this person than what I have given him credit. I look forward to spending time with him, learning all the way.

"We are ready. Time?"

"4:15, Nate dog." responded Brandon.

"Explorers: Nate Evans, Colton Lewis, Tyler Morgan, Lindsey Morgan, Brandon McClung, and Rachel . . . Rachel, what's your last name again?"

"Collins. Rachel Collins."

"Beautiful. Thank you." Nate glanced up from his notebook and made eye contact with me. His penetrating, ice blue eyes capture me. At this particular moment, I am mesmerized by him. I cannot seem to look away. I know that this is wrong and that I am here with Colton, but I can't stop admiring him. Knowing that I am in a trance, Nate smiles and whispers, "Beautiful." Terrified that someone saw that, my eyes dart around the crowd to make sure that no one has witnessed our little moment. The only possibility was Lindsey. She quickly unzipped her bag and glanced back in my direction. When my eyes met hers, she gave me a look of guilt. Fortunately, she is the quiet one today. Hopefully she'll forget about it by the end of the day.

"Remember to watch your step. If anyone gets in trouble, shout immediately. Don't hesitate." Nate gave his final instructions before turning and starting into this new tunnel. Seemingly smaller than the others, I'm wondering how in the world I will fit through.

Trying to use my best whisper tone, "Cole, how do we get through this?"

"You're going to have to get dirty. There will be some major crawling going on in here."

"I'm not scared about getting dirty, I'm scared about getting stuck."

"No, you'll be fine. If we can all fit through, so can you." he says flexing his muscles and puffing his chest out like a rooster.

"You're right. What was I thinking?" We both laughed.

Our group slithered around, crawled under, pried ourselves through crevices, boulders, and holes. I am physically exhausted. My muscles ache, I've ripped my muddy jeans, my shoes are wet and mushy, and I'm starting to shiver from the cold. Unlike the others, I am not donning the appropriate spelunking attire. My flashlight, my eyes within the cave, begins to flicker. Panic-stricken, I grab Cole's hand.

"My light is going out. Don't let go of me, Cole."

"You're okay. My flashlight is fine and I won't let you out of my sight. I promise."

After about thirty minutes, Nate came to a complete stop. We can not see what is in front of him, nor do I care to at this point. He did not say a word and he remained motionless. Brandon moved up beside him to get a closer look. Cole, Lindsey, Tyler, and I straggled behind and eventually caught up to them.

"What is it Nate? Why did you stop?"

No comments from either.

"Nate, what's . . . ?" Cole lost his words.

Before us was an enormous room, the largest chamber I've seen on this trip. It almost looked like one of the hidden chambers in an Indiana Jones movie. The center of this circular arena held a stage-like area surrounded by ten symmetrical rows of carved rock forming seats. There are three separate openings on the opposite side of the vault. What is this? What purpose would this serve? We stood there in dismay. No words were spoken. Everyone's eyes focused on the concealed, protected environment.

"What do you think this is, Nate?" asked Lindsey.

"I honestly have no idea. I've never seen anything like it in here. Let's go on in and look for carvings in the stone benches."

We all entered the room with caution, each of us heading in different directions to expedite the search. One by one we inspected the stone and its surrounding surfaces.

"I've got something over here", Brandon's voice said from across the room. We all ran over to his side and read the numbers "1863".

"What happened here in 1863?" I asked the group.

"Was that the year of the civil war battles?" Tyler added.

"You're right, Tyler. In 1863, there was a battle fought in the streets and at the Tucker farm. I remember hearing that at the war reenactment this year. What would that have to do with this place?"

"My concern isn't the date or what it has to do with this room, my question is where do those three exits lead to?" Nate, once again, showing his passion for exploration.

"Nate, you know we don't have enough time to take on all three tonight. So, what do you have in mind?" Cole was trying to keep him focused.

"I'm thinking that we need to break up into pairs, all agreeing to walk into the exit for fifteen minutes then returning with our updates. This will give an idea of which to explore next."

"I second the motion." Brandon exclaimed.

"Alright, count us in. Which entrance do you want us to go into?" Cole questioned.

"First of all, you two can't go in together. We can't wait all night for you love birds to come out of the nest. We should break up into pairs according to experience and love status. I recommend Cole and Lindsey, Brandon and Tyler, and I will take Rachel."

"No deal, Nate. She stays with me. I'm not letting her out of my sight. I made a promise." Cole was being so matter of fact. I've never seen this side of him. Very protective.

"I think she'll be okay with me for thirty minutes, besides, I need help drawing the maps. I've heard that she is one of the best art students at East."

Colton looked at me, "I'm not leaving you."

"It's only thirty minutes. I'll hang back with Nate. It's really no big deal, I can help him. Just go and hurry back."

"Are you sure? Do you feel safe?"

"I'll be fine. I'm sure that I'll be in good hands, right?"

"You won't find anyone better than Nate. He will definitely watch over you."

Nate gave each leader of the individual groups a piece of paper and a pencil for documentation. Especially when it came to something of this caliber, you have to have all of your details organized. This unexplored area was something that many archeologists would give their lives to see.

"Fifteen minutes in and fifteen minutes out. Does everyone understand that?" Nate commanded.

"Yes. Yes. Let's go Lindsey. Looks like you get to go play with me in the dark." Immediately I gave Cole a look that let him know that I didn't approve of his attempt to humor me. He just smiled and blew me a kiss. At once, they turned and entered the first exit from the room.

"Brandon, you get to play with me." Tyler puckered his lips and made kissing noises. The four of us laughed. The two boys walked into the second exit and out of sight.

"Okay, Rachel, it's our turn. I'll need you to help me draw a diagram of this passage. We can get the others later. I won't make any rude comments about being alone with me and I promise to be on my best behavior." Nate handed me a piece of paper, a pencil, and a new flashlight. I could tell that he was back to business. At least at the moment. We entered the third and final exit.

Cautiously, we walked side by side through this doorway not knowing where it would lead us. This tunnel was at least six feet wide, much larger that the crevices we had to pry ourselves through to get to the large chamber room. Unlike the rest of the cavern, this looked more like a man-made tunnel of some kind. There seemed to be a pebble or gravel covering on the floor instead of slick mud. Along the way, I drew as quickly as I could every corner and its details. Then the conversation began . . .

"So, did Cole tell you the history behind our cave explorations?"

"No, not really, just that you all came in here a lot. Can you tell me?"

Without hesitation, Nate begins, "It all started when I would go exploring by myself. I found several small crevices that I could squeeze myself through, so of course, I went in. Behind those walls, and miles of walking, I found myself under the lavish downtown of Lewisburg."

"What! You're kidding! This cave leads to the town?"

"Absolutely. Now, we just go exploring to find out what other interesting things we can discover down here. There are a lot of family secrets, hidden passages, you know, the dirt. I can't say too much right now. You are still new to the group. The time will come."

"In other words, you don't trust me."

"It's not that I don't trust you . . . I don't know you. Cole is quite smitten and he is a good judge of character, but sometimes that's not enough. You have to earn my respect."

Although his words cut through me like a knife, I could understand where Nate was coming from. This is his own personal project that he has let others take part of and he wants to make sure that everyone involved is a team player. Apparently this is serious stuff.

"Well, I hope in time you will realize that I'm not here to sabotage your project. I'm fascinated with it all. I can keep secrets and I am a good actress when I need to be. I can be trusted with anything."

"Good."

We continued walking, only about ten minutes into our trip, until Nate grabbed my arms and pushed me. His hand over my mouth and his forearm pressing my back against the frigid wall. His eyes filled with panic. I 'm not struggling against him, I am terrified.

"Shh. Be quiet. Don't move or say anything." He whispered in my ear. His face veered looking over his shoulder in the direction in which we were traveling. I could tell that he was intently watching and listening to what lies ahead of us. My heart pounding in my chest, I could feel the flow of blood as it coursed through my veins with every beat.

Again, he leans in to my ear muttering, "Do you hear that?", with his hand still over my mouth, all I can do is give him a visual affirmation by nodding my head. I can't explain what I am hearing, but I do hear something. Like a combination of running water and soft undertones of voices. The murmurs are not recognizable, nor do they sound like anyone in our group. By looking at Nate's face, I can tell that he is baffled.

"I'm going to remove my hand from your mouth. You stay right here and I'm going in for a closer look. Do not follow me. Stay here. I'll be right back."

I stood with my back against the wall unable to move. I watched Nate vanish around the corner and out of sight. Terrified; alone, my thoughts wandered. What was this noise we are hearing? Where are the others? What if Nate doesn't return? He has the flashlight. I am basically abandoned.

A shuffling noise then catches my attention. Being in complete darkness, I try to focus my eyes in the direction of the rustle. I hear what sounds like footsteps, closer and closer. Fear overwhelms me and my body begins to tremble. My hands shaking, my lips quivering, my knees weakening, all I can do is wait to see who approaches. Suddenly, nothing. Silence. An unnatural, chilled draft lingers around me. Shivering and frightened, I cross my arms and crouch down as I press my spine further into the cavern wall. This presence still encompasses me. Hair on my arms and back of my neck begins to stand on end. It feels as if someone or something is beside me, but I am sightless. An audible sigh and a brush of frigidness against my arm, makes me jump. Immediately I am standing, but unable to run due to disorientation. Extending my arms out trying to touch whatever is before me.

In a whispering gasp I hear, "help me". The tone is that of a female but is not familiar. I do not respond. Standing in shock, I am unable to think.

"Lindsey?" I murmured.

Silence.

"Who are you?"

"Come." sighed the voice.

"I can't see. Where are you?" My hands are frantically feeling the space in front of me, but all I can perceive is an unexplained coolness. Realizing that I could be dealing with something supernatural, I panic. Stumbling over a huge rock beside me, I begin back towards the main chamber. I keep one hand on the tunnel and the other outstretched before me. Confused and disoriented, I sit down on the floor bracing myself against the passageway.

Again, I hear footsteps approaching. A shuffling, hurried gate in manner.

"Rachel?" a male voice inquired.

"Nate, is that you?"

"Where are you? I dropped my flashlight, Rachel."

"Keep coming towards my voice. I'm scared, Nate. Where were you?"

While Nate touched my shoulder, I could feel him stoop down beside me. Placing his arm around my shoulder, he tries to comfort me. His breathing swift and shallow.

"What did you do run all the way here?"

"Yeah, pretty much. I went back to where I had left you and you weren't there. I panicked and dropped my light. All I heard was glass shatter and then there was darkness. Realizing that you were alone with nothing, I tried to get back to you as soon as I could. Are you okay?"

"Just a little shaken. Did you hear anything?"

"No, I went deeper into the cave, but there was nothing there. It actually looks like the tunnel leads out of the cave. Maybe someone was standing near the exterior entrance. Why?"

"Nothing."

"Rachel, you are shaking. What happened?"

"Between you and me. Do not repeat this to anyone."

"You have my word. I promise." Nate agreed.

"When you were gone, I heard a shuffling noise. I thought maybe it was you. Then, I felt this extreme coldness around me. There was a female voice telling me to "help her". I thought maybe it was Lindsey. When she didn't respond to me, I quickly moved from there. I was terrified. Hearing you, I thought maybe someone was chasing me. Were you playing a prank? Was that you?"

"No, Rachel, that wasn't me. I had walked towards the end of the tunnel then hurried back, like I said before. Did she say anything else to you?"

"Other than a sigh, she had told me to come."

"Come where?" Nate replied.

"I'm not sure. That's when I startled myself thinking that I was dealing with something spooky and left."

"Did she give you a name?"

"No, Nate. Why are you asking me this?"

Nate didn't comment but stood to his feet and grabbed my hand so I would do the same. Placing my face in both of his hands, he said to me, "Don't be scared. You are protected."

"Protected? What are you talking about?" I said, swiftly removing his hands.

"We'll talk about this later."

I could hear him turning to leave towards our destination. I clutched his arm demanding his full attention, "No, we'll talk about this now. Between you and Cole, this secrecy is driving my crazy. First there's Sarah then there's this. I've had enough."

"Sarah. Did you say Sarah?"

"Yes, Sarah."

"How do you know her?" Nate questioned.

"I had an accident one day and my mother said that someone named Sarah contacted her. I don't know anyone by that name. Do you?"

"Amazing. Where was the accident?"

"Persinger Farm, why? Do you know Sarah?" I asked again.

"What did Cole tell you?"

"He said we would talk about it later. He said that the Sarah he knew was not a student at East. That's all I know."

"I think he has to be the one to tell you, not me."

"Give me a break. This is ridiculous! I just confided in you about what I just went through and you can't trust me with a little information about some girl."

"I can't. It's a matter of respect."

"Cole's old girlfriend? Your old girlfriend? What is it Nate? Enlighten me." At this point, I am standing directly in front of Nate. My face is so close to his that I can feel his breath against my skin. Preoccupied by anger, I am unaware of the audience that has approached from the corridor.

"She was my sister!" a voice bellowed from the group.

One by one, flashlights turned on and the faces of our friends emerged. Each person turning to look towards Colton, the brother who had spoken.

"So much for sneaking up on you two and scaring you." Tyler said.

"Cole, you told me that you were an only child."

"Am I not?"

"So, you had a sister?"

"Yes, an adopted sister."

"So, what happened to her?" I pleaded.

"Cole, we're going out. This is a private conversation. I'll wait for you guys in the shop. Take your time." Nate commented. "Let's go."

Painfully, I stared into Cole's eyes. He was lost in thought, or memories for that matter. He couldn't look at me so I realize that I had touched upon something painful for him. He walked over and motioned for me to sit down with him. I reached for his hands to try and comfort him before his speech began. Fearing the worst, I took in a deep breath and exhaled slowly.

"This is not something I like talking about."

"Then don't. You tell me when the time is right."

"You are in this with us and you deserve the truth." Colton squeezed my hand as he contemplated what he would say next. "My parents adopted a girl older than me. Her parents were killed in an automobile accident out on Snake Run Road in Alderson. Not far from here. She lived with us for several years, then one day she was gone."

"What do you mean gone?"

"My mother said that on the day she left that they had a heated argument and she walked out the door. Days later, a mailman found parts of her shirt and a shoe in the culvert downtown. The sheriff told us that she must have run away and was abducted. We looked for weeks, contacting other counties and putting posters everywhere. She never came home and her body was never found. Eventually, everyone stopped looking for her."

"Did your mom not chase after her to try and stop her?"

"No."

"Why didn't people continue searching? I would think that you would keep looking until she was found alive or dead."

"Time just passed. I thought maybe it was because she couldn't deal with the tragedy of her parents untimely passing. They were friends of the family and both were business partners with my father at his, well their, law firm. Very prominent people. She wasn't the same after the wreck. Even though my family legally adopted her, she never would agree to change her name. That seemed to upset my parents, but I understood her needing to keep her own identity."

"So, what is her name?"

"Her name was Sarah Forde." Cole states wistfully.

With the mention of her name, a cool breeze rushes up my spine and chills my soul. Carefully, I inhale in silence so that Colton does not notice my restlessness. An uncomfortable awareness closes in around our two bodies.

"How horrible it must have been for her. Losing her parents, adjusting to a new family, I cannot imagine the pain." I watched Cole closely. I couldn't read his thoughts. He seemed reluctant about speaking of this occurrence. He constantly looked from side to side carefully choosing his words before spoken. Could he sense this unfamiliar presence?

"Cole, why do you think it is the same Sarah? It could be another one, you know."

"I don't know, that's the problem. This is all too overwhelming. When you first said the name, I automatically thought of her. We haven't seen her in town, but maybe she's hanging around somewhere close by."

"But why would she and I be at the farm? Why would she be with me? I have no connection with her."

"I have no idea. It's probably not her, just the name, it brought back lots of memories."

We stood in silence for several minutes. Realizing that I need to tell him about my experience in the cave, I contemplate the words to be spoken. Unfortunately, there is only one way to say it and that would be the direct and honest route.

"I have to tell you that while Nate and I were in the cave, something happened."

"What! What did he do? I thought I could trust him!" My words had led Cole into a rage. His fists clinched by his sides, lips pursed, neck muscles strained; his impetuous, unexpected temper startles me.

"No, no. Not between us. He had walked away from me for a few minutes and in the alone time in the dark, someone spoke to me. She said "help me" and "come". I was terrified. I thought maybe it was Lindsey or Nate playing a joke on me, but it wasn't either of them."

Colton, felling more at ease, looked down at the dirt while moving pebbles with his feet. Making circles, he crossed his arms and tears filled his eyes. As he looked up to me, I could feel his distress. A heaviness filled the air around us. I placed my arm around his shoulder to comfort him. Gently, I wiped a tear from his cheek while leaning closer to kiss his forehead. At that moment, Cole looked up making eye contact, touching my face and sliding his hand around to the back of my neck and carefully pulled me closer to him. His other hand, now brushing against my cheek and lifting my head, gradually came to rest with the other behind my neck and in my hair. His breathing accelerated, we are both eager and feeling the passion that is shared between us. For days since our first meeting, there was a immediate connection. This is the moment I have been waiting for. I don't care if we are in a damp, smelly cave for our first kiss.

"May I?" Cole whispered.

"Please."

Our lips met without delay, such sweetness and fragility. Cole' s lips so soft and inviting. I realize that he has had experience in kissing girls; his face, his hands, I become his student. Submissive and optimistic, I am not opposed to staying here with him for the rest of my life. The moment surpasses my finest daydream. Several minutes pass filled with intense emotion and craving. Until finally, without any warning, Cole withdrew his hands from hair advancing them to my face. He explored my cheek bones, my chin, my parted lips, as we simultaneously broke from our embrace. My eyes still closed longing for an encore.

"Beautiful." Cole said sarcastically.

"What?"

"Beautiful." he said smirking.

"You caught that earlier? Why didn't you say something?"

"Because you fidget under pressure. Why do you think that I agreed to let you go with Nate. I like watching you squirm. There is such a luscious innocence about you."

"You are such a game player. Why do you do that to me?"

"Because I like you."

"Do you really?"

"Absolutely."

"Or am I just someone to help pass the time."

"If I want to pass time, I can hang out with the guys. There is something about you. I can't explain it. Something special."

Since the whole mood had taken a change for the best, I thought it would be an opportune time to change the subject to something less dreary.

"We' ll finish our conversation later. Let's get out of this cold, dark cave. I need to get home. My mom will worry about where I am. Besides, I've played with you in the dark enough today." Laughing, we walked hand in hand within the cave, helping each other through the crevices and tunnels. Ascending towards the bright, white light, I savor the caving experience. This has been the best day of my life. My very first kiss is with Colton Lewis, Mr. Lewisburg.

Feeling like a mole coming out of its natural habitat, I squint my eyes trying to reacquaint myself to the world we are reentering. As we strolled through the doorway, Nate can be seen sitting at his desk working diligently on his new exploration. Not even looking up he begins his conversation.

"So, did you two kiss and make up?"

I immediately felt my cheeks blush at the sound of the word kiss. Emotions flourish towards the surface and I cannot contain the smile that has permanently formed on my face.

"Yes, you can say that. Thanks for bringing the others out. We needed time alone to get a few things settled."

"No problem, man. You should know by now that I would do anything for you. Anything." With saying that, Nate looked up at Cole and gave him a discerning glance that made for an uncomfortable moment.

"I know that, Nate. And I would do the same." Cole starred back in his direction. There was an enormous amount of tension and anxiety filling the space around us. Feeling like I was witnessing two lions preparing to fight for leader of the pride, I took several steps towards the exit door.

"Am I missing something? Is this a coded conversation?"

"No, you haven't missed anything, Rachel, you just might not have caught on to it?" Nate claimed.

"Nate, that's enough!" Cole growled.

"What's wrong? Did you not tell her everything that we've come up against here in Lewisburg? How your sister has been messing with our heads for months now? I've been sitting here waiting for you two to come out of the cave, worrying that I might have to go back in to find you if she decides to get revenge."

"Me, why would I need revenge?" I questioned Nate.

"Not you, darlin, I'm talking about Sar . . . ."

"Nate, that's enough, I said!" Cole jumped across the desk to confront Nate positioning himself face to face with his provoker. "Let it go, man. Don't do this." Cole, grasping Nate's shoulders, in a pleading fashion, trying to convince him to back down. Suddenly, Nate pushes him away and glares at the two of us.

"If you are going to bring her into the group, you need to come clean with that girl and let her know what we're up against." Nate demanded.

"I will, I promise." Cole looked in my direction immediately following that comment then back to Nate. "So, are we good?"

"When you tell her, we will be." Nate walked towards me standing by the door, stopped directly in front of me and said, "Welcome to the club." as he passed. With that, he opened the door giving us a look to let us know that it was time for us to leave. Quietly, we joined the others outside. Everyone must have overheard the conversation, because all eyes were on the three of us leaving the building. None of them would make eye contact with me. Not even Tyler.

"I'm going to review everyone's notes and drawings, so in a few days, if you all want to go back in, we will. Just let me know who is willing to go." Nate informed.

"You know that we're in, Nate. Just tell us when." Brandon replied. Nate climbed into his Jeep, Brandon following behind as expected. The two of them drove off in a large cloud of dust.

"Don't pay any attention to him, Cole. You know how he gets all wrapped up into this adventure thing." Tyler said comforting.

"He speaks the truth. I've only attempted to deny the things that he is trying to discover. It'll be fine. We're good. We're all good." He looks in my direction as he walks to my side of the car and opens the door. "Let's go, Sunshine. We need to make a quick stop before I take you back to your car."

Following orders, I waved to Lindsey and Tyler, while climbing into the car. I didn't question where we were traveling to, knowing that we would be going there regardless of my concern. Traveling at a high rate of speed towards town, I looked at Cole's face, stern and rigid, with such focus. He is definitely on a mission. Destination unknown to me. There was no conversation between the two of us. I'm not sure what just happened at the cave and I'm not wanting to start an argument.

"Here we are." Cole commented matter-of-factly.

I look up and before me is a cemetery. There is a large, white brick and stone church before us. The whole back of this church is the resting place of hundreds of people: old tombstones their markers. Many of these were practically fallen over and eroded from years of weather.

"What is this?" I said.

"This is a cemetery, Rachel."

"Really? I would have never of known that." I sarcastically commented, "I see that it is a cemetery, but why are we here?"

"I need to show you something. Nate is right. I need to let you in on a few things." Cole looks in my direction expressionless.

We park along the road located on the side of the church. By this time, it is quickly getting dark and I'm apprehensive about his little adventure. He takes a flashlight from his glove box and motions for me to exit the car. Filled with uncertainty, I open the door and step out onto the sidewalk. Cole meets me as we begin walking side by side towards an opening in the fence.

"Will you tell me why we are here?"

"Just keep walking. I'll explain everything in a few minutes. There is no reason to be scared. No one here will hurt you. They are all sleeping." A smile emerges on his face.

"I really do not like cemeteries. I'm a firm believer that this is a sacred place and people should not come here unless they are visiting loved ones." I pleaded my case.

Cole did not comment, he only continued walking to the rear of the church towards a plot with an angel statue standing all alone. Isolated, fairly new compared to the others, angelic hands extended to the sky. Fresh flowers laid at the angel's feet; lilies and tulips, my favorite.

"We are here to see a loved one." he replies. His face drops as his eyes filled with tears. I am uncertain as to why Cole feels the need to show me the resting ground of his ancestors. How romantic could that possibly be? This is my dead Grandfather Edward, his wife Katherine, and these are my parent's plots when they pass . . . Boy, he sure does know how to keep a girl on her toes.

As I look at the stone on the ground it reads, "Sarah Elizabeth Forde".

"This is Sarah? You told me that she was never found? Did you lie to me?"

"I know what I told you. It wasn't all a lie. The mailman did find her shirt and a shoe. I just didn't tell you about the bones that were found when the city was fixing the drainage area on the corner here."

"The drainage area where you can here the stream running under the town?"

"Yes. Dental records proved that it was Sarah." Tears flowing down his cheeks, he glances up and observes my expression. He can probably read the disappointment and dismay I am feeling at the moment. "Please say something. Tell me you hate me for not telling you everything. Tell me that you think I'm crazy for chasing a ghost."

"Chasing a ghost? What are you taking about?"

"Please call your mom and let her know that you're okay and tell her that we're going to get something to eat. You'll be home later. I'll follow you to make sure that you get home. This is going to take a while and I need to get if off my chest tonight."

Following directions, I do as I'm told. My mother, excited that I'm actually spending time with other teenagers, gives her approval and tells me to take my time, but not to be out too late. Immediately, I start the conversation again.

"You need to tell me everything."

"Construction workers found the bones. DNA and dental records concluded that it was Sarah. No one could figure out how she got down inside the drainage because it takes heavy equipment to move the metal barrier. We all knew that the shirt and shoe must have been washed out with the heavy rainstorms of spring. It's been a mystery ever since."

"But, why do you say that you are chasing ghosts?"

"I have to tell you about this angel statue first. This will help you understand. What ever you do, do not look into the eyes of the statue."

"What?" Of course, with curiosity, my eyes glance down towards the angel's face.

"Don't!" Colton grabs my face between his hands in a jerking motion lifting my head.

"That hurt!"

"Just listen. I'm sorry. I didn't mean to hurt you, but follow directions, will you?"

"Yes, yes." I pout, "Go on."

"Every October, usually around Halloween, there is a local tour of the haunted homes and buildings here in Lewisburg. Last October, the guide decided to bring the group here to Sarah's grave and made up some story about the girl in the ground. Something about a murder. Well, one of the men decided to take a closer look at the statue. He told the others that as he peered into the angel's eyes, he saw his life flash before him and actually saw his death. No one thought much of it and thought that he was trying to play tricks on the others to vamp up the storyteller's tall tale. Well, within one week, he was dead. Coincidence? Who knows. Then the following week, the guide tells this story about how the man looked into the angel's eyes and died soon thereafter. So, what happens? A young lady in this group decided that she is a non-believer and decides to tempt her fate. She too tells her group that she saw her life up to this point and that she saw her death; a tragic car crash. Within the month, her car is hit by a tractor trailer truck and there is nothing left of her. Coincidence? The list goes on and on. Fortunately, many locals now respect the statue and we don't bother her."

"Sarah? Why would she kill people?"

"We don't think that it's Sarah killing people, but there is definitely something unsettling going on here. It's like her spirit needs peace."

"Do you think she was murdered?"

"Apparently her neck was broken. Could she have fallen or was she killed? No one knows and no one cares. It's like Sarah was forgotten. That's when our little group was formed and got involved. We decided one weekend to go camping in the cave. With enough supplies to last for several days, we hiked deep within the cave. After many twists and turns, we discovered that the cave and stream flows under the town and under many homes and businesses. We've actually tried to see if we could enter these places from the cavern below, but there must be some kind of barricade blocking the entrances. We could not enter the doorways. We're not sure which building is where but we know they are there."

"How do you know?"

"Sewage."

"Sewage?" I wrinkle my nose at the grotesque sound of the word.

"I know, it's gross, but when these homes were built back in the 1830's, septic systems were not required. It was easier for the homeowners to dump their sewage into the cave. Wouldn't bother anyone, right? It would just wash away into the stream. There were no environmentalists to complain to the government."

"So, what did you all do?"

"We just keep exploring. We try to see where else this cave leads. If Sarah was murdered, where did they bring her in at?"

"Is that why Nate freaked out today? Does he think that it was Sarah's spirit talking to me?"

"Yes. For some reason, IF it is her, she is drawn to you."

"She told me to help her and to come with her. Where do you think she was wanting me to go?"

"I'm not sure. I do know that she left swiftly when Nate came back, right? So, she must want you alone."

"Okay, Colton, that freaks me out."

"I don't think that Sarah would ever hurt anyone. She had a good soul."

"She might have been a good soul here, but what about where she is now?"

"I just can't see it. At this point, I don't know what to do. Maybe she is trying to give us the answers that I have been searching for. I want her to have peace. To rest in peace."

Realizing that I was now a part of a secret larger than this town could fathom, I apprehensively say, "What can I do to help?"

Cole grabs my hands and leans in to kiss my forehead, "That's my girl. I knew that I could count on you. Just remember that this must stay within our group. You can't tell anyone anything! This is between us."

"Yes, I understand. I'll do anything for you, you know that, don't you?"

"Well, I was hoping." Again, he kisses my forehead and gives me a comforting hug. "First things first, do you want to come to my house for a minute? I need to pick up something."

Apprehensively, I agree to go, knowing that my mother would not approve. I was taking a chance here that could ruin my opportunity to ever see this boy again. "Okay, but we need to hurry. I do not want to face the wrath of Lyn if she finds out that I went uninvited."

"You are being invited! This is your formal invitation. What do you need a fancy card in an envelope requesting an R.S.V.P.?"

"You should be a comedian. Your talent overwhelms me. Yes, you know how high maintainance that I can be. I demand a formal invite. Isn't that what people of your society do? Parties and frilly cards?"

With a look of dismay, Cole's eyes widen as he turns completely to face me. With one quick motion he tackles me with such force that I have no idea what just happened. I did not realize how offensive my comment must have been. My face in the grass and his body pressing against me, I cannot catch my breath.

"Will you be quiet for once? Look over to your right. Do you see that?"

Turning my head, I notice that there are two people arguing on the other side of the cemetery. They were looking down towards the ground screaming profanities at each other. A heated discussion indeed. Not being familiar with anyone in the town, but the few friends I have met, I have no idea who we are watching perform this great skit. Feeling as if we were intruding, I asked if we should leave.

"Would you like it if I left you or one of your friends while you were in a fight with someone? That wouldn't be a very polite thing to do. Am I right?"

"Question number one, can we at least get off the ground? Question number two, do you know that person?"

"We can get up, but let's stand over there behind the trees. And yes, I do know that person. That is my friend, Kamryn. I don't think you've had the honor of meeting her yet. She is one of the elite. She is one of the cheerleaders from school. I cant leave her, I'm not sure who she's with. His back is turned." Holding out his hand, he helps me to my feet. We walk quietly to a group of pines located on the side of the church. Luckily, there is an old wooden bench which will make a nice place to sit. Anything is better than having your body pressed against the cold, damp earth. Holding my hand, Cole gently leads me over to the bench and motions for me to sit.

"So why do you feel the need to protect this girl?" I asked.

"It's a long story."

"Well, shorten it."

"Kamryn was one of Sarah's friends. She came to our house practically every day. She grew very close to our family, but after Sarah's disappearance, we did not see her that much. I don't believe that she could handle the situation. She is a very sensitive person."

"How could you just stop visiting a family that you were attached to? That makes no sense at all to me."

"We assumed that she just needed her space. No one questioned her motive."

"Do you think that she knows something? If she was close to Sarah, would she not know details about her life? Maybe know what her schedule was the day that she disappeared? Did anyone question her about that particular day?"

"Are you interrogating me? Do I need to contact my lawyer?"

"Even a little sarcasm brings out the best in you." We both chuckled.

At that moment, we heard a girls voice coming from across the yard.

"Do not threaten me, Tristan! I told you before that I would not say anything to anybody. Why do you feel the need to threaten me? Don't you understand that if you pressure me that I might tell someone your secrets?" More words were exchanged, but we could not hear because of the rumbling of the cars passing by.

"You are smarter than that Kamryn. Walk away from him." Cole whispered quietly under his breath. We watched the two stay engaged in the conversation and finally depart in different directions.

"We need to follow her to make sure that she makes it home. Well, safely, of course. She lives two homes down from mine." Cole explains, "That's Tristan McClung, Brandon's cousin. You can't trust that boy."

"Will he see us?"

"Does it matter? What's more important, a neighbor's safety or a boy's curiosity?"

"You're right. Let's go." We slowly walked back to the car keeping an eye towards Kamryn as she emerged from the cemetery onto the main road. A beautiful girl, long blond hair and athletic build. I could see her hair glistening under the street lights as she crossed each intersection. We followed her secretly as she walked to her home. Crossing each street with caution, she kept a steady pace until she stopped in front of one of the store windows.

"What is she doing? What is she looking at?" I asked bewildered.

"I'm not sure. Maybe we should pick her up."

"Now, that would be odd. I guess we could tell her that we were spying on her at the cemetery and thought we would finish the evening by stalking her. That should go over well."

"Ok, bad idea." We pulled over against the curb as we watched her peer through the storefront window. In a trance—like motion, she reached for the door handle to enter. With one quick twist, she disappeared into the building. As we watched in dismay, we noticed a second figure approaching. It was Tristan. He paused briefly at the entrance, looked around to see if anyone noticed him, and slipped into darkness.

"This is bizarre, Cole. Do you think she will be okay?"

"Honestly, I do not know. Why are they entering her father's bakery at this time of night?"

"Maybe she forgot something? Maybe they are cleaning? I don't know Colton, let's go."

"Maybe, just maybe, she doesn't know that he's following her and she is about to get killed."

"Colton Lewis! That is a horrible thing to say! What do you expect us to do?"

"Follow them." he said sternly.

"Somehow I knew you were going to say that." The concerned expression on his face revealed his true emotions and at that point I knew we would be observing these two individuals closer. Lowering my head in disbelief, all I could do was mumble, "lead the way". Swiftly, Cole leaned over, kissed my cheek, and reached for his door.

"Game on. Let's go!" He sprung from the car and raced across the shadowy street. Leaping through the air, feet barely touching the pavement, his movements were precise. He reminded me of a wild jungle cat pursuing its prey. Thirst for danger; anticipation for the battle that lies ahead. Pressing himself against the large brick building, all I could see was two, immense white eyes and an arm waving frantically in my direction.

"You've got to be kidding me." I murmured. Following his lead, I open the door to accompany my friend, the crazed jungle cat. With the darkness comes a disturbing stillness in this small town. I can hear the stoplights changing, the cars in the distance, dogs barking, and running water beneath the street. The community seemed to be asleep and me, I must be in a dream.

Approaching the door, Cole peered through the window to see if the intruders were visible.

"I don't see them. There is a small flickering light in the back of the shop. I need to get a closer look."

I turned my head to look towards my mother's shop which was two doors down to make sure that she was not observing our behavior. "Ok. Now we will be trespassing. Do you honestly believe that is a good idea?" Silence . . . "Cole?" Nothing. I realize that I am alone. The door is ajar and there is no sign of Cole. I have to make a choice. I can choose to follow him or sit on the sidewalk and wait for his return.

Decisions, decisions. I don't want Cole to think that I'm not adventurous but I don't want him to think that I am starving for his attention either. Even though I am. I must follow his lead.

Advancing through the door, I notice that this shop has a layout much like my mother's. Visible only by the streetlights, I see the patron's sitting area located to the right of the entrance. A long narrow deli case displaying the baked goods is to my left. Several round tables are placed sporadically throughout the room. The scent of bread and spices fills the air. Quietly, I venture towards the back where I can see a small glimmer of light. Attempting to slink across the wooden floor, audible cracking sounds beneath my feet. I begin to focus on each step. My breathing deepens with fear as I approach the back storeroom or at least that's what is at our shop.

As I approach the light, I can hear voices, but cannot distinguish what is being said. There is a closet beside the entrance and that's where I decide to watch and eavesdrop. Cole is no where in sight. He has concealed himself well.

"Is someone there?" A fragile voice emerges from the room. "Hello?"

"Noone is here, Kamryn. Stop wasting time. Do it!" a deep voice growled.

"Tristan, you need to back off. I told you that I wouldn't say anything. You boys and your secrets. Do not come here to threaten me. Do you know how much trouble you are in if I decide to tell?"

"Just open the door! I'm not waiting forever. Either open it or I'll do it myself." Objects are being moved across the wooden floor. Apparently heavy objects. I can hear them pushing with force. After several minutes, utter stillness. What are they doing?

Suddenly, I can hear the sound of a crow bar prying nails from wood. I can hardly tolerate the wrenching noise of the deteriorating wood being mutilated and splintered into small pieces. Each piece of wood, one by one, detached in a slow, continuous motion.

"Tristan, are you sure about this?"

"Shut up! I told you that we have to go in there. You and me. Look, there's nothing to be afraid of. We have a flashlight and your father thinks we are at the movies. Quit being so dramatic!"

"What if its true?"

"Then it's true. Let's go." Next, shuffling feet and the light disappears.

I move secretly towards the entrance of the room. My hands outstretched trying to feel my way through the dim room. No longer can I hear Kamryn and Tristan. There must be a back door. Why our shop doesn't have one, I'm not sure.

"Cole", I whisper. "Are you in here?" I continue further for a closer examination. Inside this confined room, there is a stagnant odor that overwhelms me. A frigid numbness apprehends my sense of perception. This feeling is something familiar to me. I cannot explain my reaction or why I am so intrigued by this unique fragrance that encompasses my surroundings. Unbalanced, I turn in an attempt to leave the room, stumbling over several pieces of fragmented wood, and fall to the floor.

I raise my head to ask, "Is someone here?" With that comment a cold breeze pierces through my skin. I shiver with fear. My pulse races, my heart pounds uncontrollably within my chest. I realize at this moment that I am not alone. There is a presence surrounding me.

"Come." a soft, shallow voice whimpered. I glance around the room and see nothing.

"Where are you?" I pleaded.

"Come." The voice said more assertively from within the dark corridor. I rose to my feet and started to enter the doorway. I'm not sure where I am going or what lies ahead, but I do know that this voice is persistent. Stepping across the broken fragments of wood, I can hear muffled tones in the distance. This appears to be a tunnel. Echoing footsteps ahead of me sloshing through puddles. Water that has emerged from the ceiling descending down the corridor walls. The dampness engulfs the entire passageway. Breathing becomes a not only a necessity, but a challenge. I take another step into the darkness.

"What are you doing?" Cole asked.

Twirling back towards the entrance, there stands Cole with an inquisitive expression on his face. His eyes narrowed, his lips pursed, he doesn't look too happy. I realize that I need to respond, but I am reluctant to find the right words.

"I was looking for you."

"You were looking for me? I've been outside. How did you get in here?" Cole questioned.

"You left the door open and I followed you."

"Rachel, I've been outside. I thought I heard something in the alley and when I came back, you were gone. I waited a few minutes then I saw movement in here. Where is Kamryn and Tristan?"

"Well, that's it. I believe they went into this tunnel. Have you been in there before?" I asked.

"We've explored the tunnel under Lewisburg, but have never been able to get inside the stores. Are they still in there?"

"They haven't came out."

"Do you want to take a look? I'll do my best to behave." Cole flashed his charming smile. Now, my body with flushed with desire. It's amazing how this boy can just speak a few words to me and my whole body responds this way.

"I'll go only if you DON'T behave." I gave him a quick wink, flipped my hair, and in I went.

Quickly, he grabbed me around my waist to turn me around, "Are you giving me an ultimatum?"

Cole starred deep into my eyes. Even though it was dim, I could see his piercing eyes look straight through me. He firmly placed both of my hands behind my back and forced my body against the wall. I did not try to resist him, his power stimulates my conscience. With one hand holding my arms behind me, Cole extends his other hand to raise my chin to expose my neck. I can feel his breath on my skin. Gently, he begins to kiss my neck. The combination of his tongue and the wetness against my skin obviously facilitates extreme pleasure. He removes his grasp from behind and trails his hand from my waist to my shoulder, ever so slowly manuevering across every curve on my body. I tremble with anticipation. He glances into my eyes as his finger caresses my parted lips. His attention is directed to my lips as he watches intently as a child does with a new toy. Nervously, I bite my bottom lip.

"I love when you do that", Cole breathed deeply. "May I?" he asked.

"You have to ask?" I said eagerly. At this point, I was his captive.

Cole placed both hands on the side of my face and delicately touched my lips against his. His fingers becoming entangled in my hair with the movement of our faces. His grip was firm but not overbearing. He was in complete control and he knew it. Teasingly, he bit my lip. Realizing that he was provoking me, I broke his hold and shoved his back against the wall. A look of astonishment from the unexpected attack came across his face. Raising up on my toes, I placed my nose against his neck, breathing deeply to endure his distinctive scent. With my moist lips, I brush them against his neck, tasting him as a delicacy. Feeling a deep inhalation, I realize that Cole is enjoying my assertiveness, so I place my hands on the inside of his shirt to feel his bare chest. Rippled muscles forming a beautiful playground of goodness. My fingertips move within each groove, feeling the softness of his skin. His breathing deepens with every stroke of his chest. Control has switched hands, literally.

"Oh my gosh!" I exclaimed.

"What? What's wrong?" Cole asked bewildered.

"I'm vibrating." I said matter of factly.

"Well, I've never heard it called that before?"

"No, in my pocket. My phone. It's vibrating." I reached inside my pocket to see who was interrupting our moment. Mom, of course. She must have a "make out radar". Not that anything major would happen, but kissing this boy is amazing! "We have to go, it's mom. I'm sorry."

"Sorry? Don't be sorry. I loved every minute of you taking advantage of me." smirked Cole.

"What? I did not. I was just giving you a taste of your own medicine. You always tease me."

"I do, don't I? It just keeps you wanting more, right?"

Yeah, I want more alright. I want a relationship with this passionate, hot boy. He has consumed my thoughts every day. When he is near me, nothing else matters. When he kisses me, the world stops.

"Do you want more?" Colton questioned.

"I'm not sure how to answer that? I'm not ready for THAT."

"NO, I mean a relationship."

"With who?"

"With Scary Jerry, the town flasher . . . ME, girl. Don't you listen?"

"I don't know what to say? I never thought that you would . . ." I was interrupted by Cole planting another kiss on my lips. There is so much running through my head. I need to get home, I want to stay with him longer, he needs to kiss me again, where did Kamryn and Tristan go, what am I going to tell mom?

"Hello, Rachel? Did you hear what I said?"

The only answer I have . . . . Still not listening . . . .

"We need to go, Colton. What do we do about Kamryn?"

"I don't know. I hate to leave her in the tunnel not knowing what is happening. Call your mother and tell her you will be a little late. Think of something creative."

I realize that the right thing to do is to wait for this girl to emerge from the tunnel, but lying to my mother will not be easy. I have to conjure up a practical reason for my tardiness to reassure her that I am not doing anything scandalous. Doesn't every teenager trespass on weekends and stalk unsuspecting strangers?

The phone rings. My stomach churns with anxiety. My mind swiftly seeks an explanation to justify my obligations. After the fourth ring, Lyn answers.

"Hey, mom. It's me."

"Hey, Rachel. Where are you?"

"We just left the caves a little bit ago and now everyone is meeting for dinner, but there is a wait at the restaurant. Can I still go, please? I wont be long."

"Who are you with?" my mother asked.

"At the moment, Cole. The young man from the farm incident."

"Oh, well, isn't that nice. And how is that fine, young man this evening?"

"Mom. He's fine. Can I stay out later, please. I will be with the group, so you don't have to worry. Please?"

"Ok, Rachel. Please be home before midnight. That will give you several hours with your new friends."

"Thanks, mom! You are the greatest!"

As I glance in Cole's direction, he gives me a thumbs up gesture and an enormous grin to humor me. His exaggerated response reveals his intentions. I need to prepare myself for an epic experience like no other.

"Now we need to get serious. Let's go into the tunnel to track down the other two."

"So when we find them, what are we to say, Cole?"

"We wont have a discussion. We will observe; not communicate. We need to focus on her safety."

"Got it. Let's go." With that, we reentered the dim passageway. I could no longer hear the voices ahead of us. Unsure of our surroundings, I grasped Cole's hand to provide me with a sense of security. He squeezes gently for the reassurance I am desiring.

Similar to the caverns, this tunnel appears narrow with small piles of debris along the jagged walls. As we descend deeper into the darkness, I slide my finger tips across the cool, rough edges. Our feet shuffle through the small pebbles and stones as the floor gently slopes toward our new destination. Destination unknown. Cole removes a compact flashlight from his pocket to illuminate our path.

"Look at that," Cole says pointing to a row of doors along the side wall. "I wonder where those doors lead to?"

"Entrances into other businesses? Why would there be a tunnel underground connecting the stores?" My curiosity was overpowering my common sense.

Cole replied, "I've always heard rumors of an underground trading system when my great grandparents were alive. There was a system between the local banks and other merchants. Some even said that the tunnels were used with slavery. Even prostitution. I never had any idea that something was actually down here under the streets. I'm in awe of the complexity."

"Do you honestly believe that your ancestors traveled in these tunnels moving merchandise and even people?"

"Slavery was inhumane, but it was reality. A part of Lewisburg that many do not want to recognize. My family members were huge slave traders and bankers. Am I proud to say that they were probably in the fore front of this masquerade? No. But what my people did years ago cannot be changed. It's our history."

I was speechless. This honorable, sincere young man could not be a descendant of such despicable creatures. Slavery, yes, I know that Lewisburg is a predominately white society presently and I'm sure that years ago it probably was a mainstream for people trading. Old money and no morals.

"Say something, Rachel. Anything."

"Footprints".

"What?" Colton said puzzled.

"Oh, I'm sorry. There!" I said pointing before us, "Look at the set of footprints. They disappear behind that door." There is evidence that someone has recently entered through the wooden barrier. It appears to be several large pieces of cut timber held together by leather straps and wooden pegs. The tethered bands are showing their age with deteriorating edges and noticeable imperfections.

"What do you want to do, Sunshine? Go in or turn back?"

"As far as I'm concerned, there is no turning back now."

In deathlike silence, Cole leisurely turned the rusted handle of the door. I cringed as the heavy boards shifted across the rugged stone earth. Clinching my teeth and tightly shutting my eyes, I clutched Cole's shirt and hoped for the best. As we slipped through the entry, we were facing a wide, mustard—colored drapery. Without delay, Cole peered through the curtain to see if there was a presence within the room.

"It's all clear. We are in a storage room and there is no one here but us." Swiftly he stepped aside and lifted the curtain for me to join him.

"This is a storage room. Cole, this is . . . ," I paused to regain my composure, "Cole, this is my mother's shop." I looked frantically from side to side trying to understand why I had never seen the door behind that eye sore of a curtain. When I work at my mother's coffee shop, I enter this room, but I get what I need and leave. It scared me. The damp smell, the vast wooden shelves lining the walls, cracked concrete floor; it reminded me of my grandmother's cellar.

"What? Your mother's shop? Come on, we have to make sure that they are not destroying something." Dragging me from the room, Cole enters the hallway to the main area. Pictures of Lewisburg lined the walls. My mother was intrigued with this town and it's history. There were pictures of the North House Museum, the General Lewis Inn, several historic homes, people from every walk of life, old and young, and some from the Civil War Era. She has even placed pictures of our ancestors from years past on the walls from someplace unknown. Her epic collection is mainly derived from the historian at the museum that she dated for several months. Every evening we heard about this town and it's mysteries. Pictures and memories.

"But why would they come in here? It's a coffee shop! I love mochas, but I wouldn't trespass to get one!"

"You're right." Investigating the room, we see no signs of anyone. Complete silence. We look behind the counter, under tables, around corners, behind shelves, nothing. Only coffee beans, greeting cards, trinkets, jewelry, and books. A relaxing atmosphere that welcomes all who enter. The best coffee in town. Bunch of Wild Beans; tasty goodness.

"Well, we'd better get back before someone sees us in here through the window. I just don't understand. If the footprints lead in here, where are they?" Puzzling.

"We will shut the door back and go out the front. Do you have a key?"

"That sounds good to me." I reached inside my coat pocket to pull out a set of keys.

"Let me guess, this pink key that reads "princess" is a house key, this red key with flames is for your ride, and the ordinary silver key is to your mother's precious java palace. Am I right?" Cole sneered.

"No, genius. You're not as smart as you think you are. My house key is the plain silver one. My mother's shop is the red one with flames. You haven't met my mother to understand that correlation and the pink "princess" key is to my chariot. Close though, so close."

We both chuckle as we vacate the front entrance, securing the door behind us. Slowly, we stroll across the street toward Cole's car. A lustrous, ebony display of distinction.

"What's that?" I questioned pointing to the windshield? Did you get a ticket?"

"Probably. It doesn't matter. It will disappear tomorrow."

"You are so sure of that?"

"My family has friends in honorable positions. They make things happen." Cole removes the white paper from the windshield methodically unfolding his fate. Tightly folded and precisely creased, it appears more like a love letter from a scorned lover than a traffic violation from the local men in blue.

"What the hell?" Cole sounded perplexed as he deciphered the message.

"What's wrong, Cole?" I have never heard a harsh word leave his mouth, so I knew it must be something.

Looking up from the paper he says, "You better mind you own business."

"Excuse me? You do NOT talk to . . ."

"No, no, that's what this note says."

"Who do you think put that there? Kamryn and Tristan?" My only thoughts were how did they get passed us? No one had been in my mother's shop. How did they know that we were following?

"I guess. They must have access to another store and slipped by us. We need to pack up our spy gear and retreat."

"I agree. Time for me to get home."

"One more stop, pppllleeeeaaassseee. Call your mom back so she knows you are safe. Just twenty minutes more. I want you to meet my parents."

"They're still up?"

"Oh, yeah. They are usually entertaining their friends at this hour. You've met Gerald Long from school, right?"

"The principal? Yeah, why?" I questioned.

"Well, he and his wife, Janella, are always with my parents. Best friends gone wild. They are probably there now finishing off their second bottle of wine and telling old war stories. It's quite entertaining. Don't you want to be with me a little longer? In my house? I'll give you a private tour."

He is so persuasive. His piercing, intense eyes gaze from my face, down my arm to my hand resting on my lap. He gently reaches for my hand, removing it from my leg, and raising it to his lips.

Sweetly he whispers, "Don't you trust me?"

Of course I do, but at some point I won't trust myself. I remove my hand from his grasp and get my cell phone from my pocket. What do I say to mom? She knows when I'm lying. She reads me like a . . .

"Mom, hey it's me . . . . yeah, I know . . . we are all having such a great time that I was wondering if I could . . . I know . . . but . . ."

Colton snatches the phone from me and gives me one of his "I've got this" looks.

"Ms. Collins, mam, this is Cole. I wanted to personally apologize for keeping your lovely daughter out this late. My group of friends have really taken to her and we just lost track of time . . . yes, mam . . . I promise . . . thank you, mam . . . oh, I'll show her a good time. When I get her home,

I'm going to lay her down on my bed, whisper scandalous things in her ears, and caress her . . ."

I ripped the phone from his ear waiting to hear my mother screaming profanities, but all I heard was a dead silence.

"You jerk!" With quick reflexes, I hit Colton in the arm. "Ouch!" My hand throbbed in pain as it met against his brawny, tan bicep. It was like smashing into a brick wall. Solid.

"What did you do that for? Let me see it?" He begins to kiss each finger one by one.

"I thought you were saying those things to my mom. She would die!"

"I would never embarrass you that way. She hung up after giving permission for you to stay out longer. Relax. You are with me and I will take care of you."

We drive to the top of the hill past the antique shops, bank and post office. Such a quaint community. Smaller than many I have lived in. The architecture of the aged buildings, many of which are dated to the 1800's. The old town charm is depictive of its history.

"Here we are." Cole says turning into a narrow driveway. As I peer through my window, I see elegance at its best. This has to be a prank. Before us, perched on a knoll, is a grand, red brick mansion. Four, white pillars extending from the front entrance to the third level. One by one, we pass well manicured trees and flower beds lining the edges of the paved driveway. When we reach the stairs that lead to the entrance, he follows the circular path and stops at a second attached building.

"Funny. Your deception is amusing. Now, let's go to your house before the owners come out and have you arrested." I jeered.

"I don't believe they'd have me arrested for coming home early. Maybe for bringing home a stray." He flashed me that smile that I adore and sauntered to my door.

"Welcome home, Miss Collins. We have been awaiting your arrival." I extend my hand and allow Colton to assist me from the car.

"Wow. I am nervous. I knew you were wealthy, but I never imagined this. I think you should take me home now." Old habits die hard, as I begin to bite my lip.

"This neurotic fetish of lip biting is starting to turn me on." Colton says as he caresses my lip with his thumb. I bite him to let him know that he shouldn't tempt me. We both laugh.

"So what is this?" I point in the direction of the smaller building.

"That is the maid's quarters. Her name is Nancy. She has lived with us for years. She is like a second mother to me."

A maid. Great. My evening just got worse. My family lives on my mom's salary, which isn't much after she covers her expenses with the shop and his family has a mansion with a maid. Wonderful.

"Really, I don't have to meet your parents, Cole."

"I know you don't HAVE to, but I want you to. Just relax and follow my lead."

That's what I've been doing.

We saunter past the brick wall which becomes visible as we approach the cobble stone sidewalk. A large fountain is located directly in front of the walkway. Water spraying five feet in the air with hues of blue and green radiating from the lighting beneath. It reminds me of something you would see at The Greenbrier Resort. I've never been there personally, but I've seen pictures.

"Welcome to my humble abode". Cole reaches for the large pewter finished handle. I can see people through the glass of the door. I panic.

"Cole, wait. Are you sure about this?"

"I've never been more positive. My parents will love your simplicity and quirkiness. It's adorable. Please trust me."

Simple and quirky. Gee, sweep me off my feet. My facial expression must have given my thoughts away.

"I don't mean that in a bad way. Please don't interpret it that way. I'm saying that you do not have to be wealthy to be here. I like you for you. Not your financial status in the community." His flattery becomes my confidence.

I can't believe that I'm doing this, "I'm ready. Bring on the Lewis'." I clasp my fingers around his as he leads me through the door to meet the wealthiest parents of Lewisburg . . . their town.

The display before me is refined elegance. A massive chandelier hangs from the sky-high ceiling. The light fixture must be fifteen feet long. Layers of sparkling glass forming a waterfall effect, as it tapers towards the floor below. I can see three levels as the grand staircase emerges from the white, marbled entrance and extends upward in the center of the foyer area. Each level is open with only a dark wooden banister visible for those who enter.

"My parents are probably in the living room, but I want to show you around first." He affectionately gives me a reassuring smile as we advance towards the inner most part of this maze of a house. We walk through the kitchen, the formal dining room, the theatre, the exercise room, the library, and passed by seven or so bedrooms each having its own private bathroom. We ventured up and down the stairs exploring each living area. One level is the size of our entire home. I find myself shaking my head as we turn each corner not knowing what to expect next.

"Here's my room." I can say that I wasn't expecting that. We should not go in there. It is not appropriate for a young lady to enter a boy's room. Especially when it is the first visit to meet the parents.

"Very nice." I peer through the doorway into his room. The vision of Pier One before me. His bedding, in dark tones, accentuates the colossal, wooden posts that extend from each corner of the bed. An array of huge, fluffy pillows rest on the comforter. The bed looks so inviting, even if you have to put forth effort to get in it. There are three steps leading to the raised platform holding this bed. It must be a California King. It is massive. Looking around the room, I see built in, wall to wall bookshelves lined with sports memorabilia and other collectibles. To the back of the room, I can see French doors that must lead to a balcony. How romantic.

"Colton? Is that you?" a female voice came from downstairs.

"Yes, mother. It's me. I brought home a friend and I was showing her around. We'll be right down." He turned to me and said, "It's Showtime."

"May I please use the restroom first?"

"Of course, you can use mine. I'll wait here." He nudged me towards the door in the furthest part of his bedroom. "It's safe, go ahead."

Following his instruction, I walked to the back and entered his bathroom. It was as lovely as the rest of the house with marble tile and extravagant décor. I shut the door behind me and began to walk towards the opposite corner of the room. How nice it is to see how the other half lives. Looking into the mirror as I wash my hands, I get an uneasy feeling that I am not alone. I survey behind myself, but see nothing. My common sense is being overpowered by my non-sense. "Cole? Are you still there?" Nothing. As I turn to leave, I accidentally knock a towel from the counter. Bending over to pick it up, I have the experience of a frigid draft whisking by me. Startled, I lunge towards the door believing that I saw something from the corner of my eye. My body freezes. I am numb.

"Look" a ghastly voice announces.

I redirect my eyes towards the sound of my company, but all I see is a small picture frame. Upon closer examination, I recognize Cole with a girl. A lovely girl with long, dark hair and chestnut brown eyes. Absolutely stunning. They are dressed in formal attire. Must be a family party, must be one of his old girlfriends and my imagination must be going into overdrive. I laugh at myself for believing that I am having an encounter with something in my boyfriend's bathroom.

"Rachel, are you alright?" Cole calls from the opposite side of the door.

"Yes, I'm coming out now." I open the door and there he is, my prince charming.

"Can I tell you something, Rachel?"

"Sure, but can we hurry downstairs before I have a nervous breakdown?"

"You're right. Let's go. It can wait." We scurried towards the stairs.

Down the grand stairway and entering a second sitting area, there are five adults sitting before us sipping wine glasses. Cole points to two empty bottles of wine sitting on the bookcase and smiles. They appear to be engrossed in conversation and I feel like an intruder of their environment.

"Hey, Colton. Who is your friend?" his mother asked.

"Mom, Dad, Mr. and Mrs. Long, Mrs. Bennett, this is Rachel Collins. Rachel, this is my mother, father, the Longs, and a family friend, Carrington Bennett." Colton proclaimed proudly.

"Hello. It is very nice to meet all of you." I said nervously. My hands and knees were trembling. These people were out of my league and I am only kidding myself to believe that I will be accepted into their circle.

"It is nice to meet you, Rachel", Colton's father says, "where are you from?"

"Oh, I am from many places, but my family has settled here on the north end of Lewisburg. I am a transient, but not by my choice. My mother likes to get around. I mean, my mother doesn't like to be in one place too long. She enjoys her privacy and enjoys hiding behind new walls. Not that she's hiding from anyone . . ." my head was spinning.

"I think they get the point, Sunshine." Cole consoles me by placing his arm around my shoulder and squeezes gently. I exhale in relief. His parents smile as if giving their condolences.

"Cole has told us that your mother owns that enchanting coffee shop downtown. So, your mother is Lyn Collins? What a splendid family and a pleasant lady, I must say." Cole's father stated.

"Yes, Mr. Lewis, that is correct and thank you. Do you know my family? They live in Florida?" I responded.

"Please don't call us Mr. and Mrs. I realize that is the polite thing to do, but you are welcome to call us by our first names, Dylan and Emily, please. And yes, I knew of the Collins when . . ."

"So, what have you all been doing this beautiful evening?" Cole interrupted.

"Cole, that is not nice to interrupt me." Dylan turns to Rachel, "so, when did you move back from Florida? Do you like it here, Rachel?"

"Yes, sir, Mr . . . . Dylan." the room laughs at my comment. I blush uncontrollably. "My mother, sister and I have been here for several months, almost a year now."

"And as for us, you can also call us by our first names, Gerald and Janella. Only at school would I appreciate the formal title of Mr. Long, please."

"Yes, sir. Absolutely." Now that roll call was almost complete, I am feeling less anxious as they continue their conversation.

Cole walks towards the other guest that is present, "This is Carrington, she is one of my mother's dearest friends. She is the owner of the Greenbrier Spa. We will have to make arrangements for you to have a day of pampering."

"Anytime", she responds, "You know that I would do anything for you, honey." Carrington swats him on his butt. The room cackles at her flirtatious behavior.

"Oh, Carrington, will you behave. Cut that woman off, Janella." Gerald exclaims. She prances over to her seat beside Dylan and Emily. Carrington is the life of the party. Whenever she is present, you know that it will be an exciting evening. It's like a mixture of passion, flirtiness, and animalistic behavior all rolled into one gorgeous body. Quite the looker.

"Dylan, did you read in the paper where the City Council is assessing everyone on this street to reconstruct the septic systems? Too late for that, don't you believe? That's why Janella and I love living in the country on our farm. None of this political bullshit." Mr. Long argued.

"If the council wants to reinvent the wheel, let them get started. The systems are what they are. These houses were built before the environmentalists got involved. The expense of redirecting and sealing the homes will be a huge expense and time consuming." Mr. Lewis added.

Perplexed by the conversation and wondering what they were discussing, I look at Cole to take me away.

"Real Estate agents have been honest in telling buyers that there is a septic issue, but no one wants to acknowledge it until there is a new drainage problem. Why don't people ask questions before purchasing one of these vintage residences? Mrs. Long added.

"Louella Jarvis even had to appear in court the other day because of one of the buyers complaining about the septic." Mrs. Lewis recalled.

I'm not sure why I thought that I should add to the conversation, but I replied, "Louella, she is my mother's best friend. Wonderful person. Very genuine and sincere."

"Yes, she is. We purchased this house from her years ago. Such a lovely, strong minded, independent woman." said Mrs. Lewis.

"She has herself a fine looking man. I need to get myself one of those." Carrington jeered.

From around the corner, we hear, "Darlin, you have trouble keeping up with me, what would you do with another?" Jake Bennett appears.

Cole looks in his direction, "and this would be Jake Bennett, a prominent contractor at the resort, Carrington's better half."

"Better? He knows what's better." Carrington argued.

Sensing the tension in the air, I ask Emily, "So, How long have you all lived here?"

"We bought this house several years ago. It's more than we need. It's just the three of us, but when Sarah was living with us, it was appropriate for our extended family." Mrs. Lewis' eyes peered downward towards the floor. "but everything happens for a reason and we must stay focused on the present."

"Someone take that woman's drink away. We all know that after a few too many, she starts reminiscing about the past and gets carried away." Janella commented. "She and Carrington need to put down the drinks. Remember the trouble you two would get into? Do you need to be reminded?"

"Yeah, and we all know what happens to you when you've had too many too, Janella." the room breaks into laughter. "Royal flush, anyone?" Gerald scoffs.

"Well, it's been great everyone, but I need to take this lovely, young lady back to her car so she can go home. I will be back soon. Try to behave yourselves. Rachel, are you ready?" I nodded in agreement.

"We hope you come back to visit us again, Rachel. It is a pleasure to have another young soul in this house." Mrs. Lewis claimed, holding back the tears.

"Focus. Stay focused, Emily. We've had this conversation before." Mr. Long growled. At times his harsh Army temperament oozes from his pores.

Momentarily ignoring the last comments, we strolled out the front entrance to Cole's car. We told my mother twenty minutes and we were already pushing thirty. I will be in trouble. We speed through town and back to my car at the school. A red bucket of bolts parked solitary in the secluded lot. There are no lights in the parking lot. Our only lighting is from the full moon above us in the sky.

"What a beautiful night. Please drive safe, Sunshine. I'll follow you home."

"Oh, no. I'll be fine." I did not want him to see where I lived after being at his home. "Can I ask you something before I leave?"

"Sure. I'm listening, but it will cost you."

"Funny. What were your parents talking about tonight? I was confused.

"Sometimes, those crazy women have too much to drink, and then they all . . ." Cole started.

"No, the houses." I corrected.

"Oh, The homes built on Washington Street are in the Historic District. Remember when I told you that there was a stream under the town?"

"Yeah, I remember."

"Well, when these were built, there was not a large concern about septic systems or where the sewage was dumped. The decision was to simply dump the sewage from the homes beneath the surface and into the stream below to carry away the waste."

"So, everything is being dumped into the stream? Isn't that toxic?"

"Like I said, years ago, our ancestors were not as knowledgeable about these issues. I'm sure there are ramifications of these actions. Why?"

"Just curious. I'm fascinated with this underworld of Lewisburg. Streams, tunnels, I have a strong desire to learn everything."

"I have a strong desire too, but it's not to discover the secrets of Lewisburg, it is to discover the intimate, hidden existence of Rachel Collins. Now, that is a mystery."

"You never give up, do you?"

"Give up? Not in my vocabulary."

"How about persistence?"

"Persistence. Now we're talking." Colton agreed.

Colton walked to my side of the car, opening the door as he always does, and held out his hand. I grabbed it, swinging my feet from the vehicle, and standing between the car and my friend. He was not leaving any room for error. As I stood up, our bodies were pressed tightly together. His arms outstretched and pinning me with restraint against the car. Gently, he kisses my forehead and backs away to open my car door. As he turns and opens the door of my precious wheels, the crunching noise sends chills up my spine. We both look at each other and laugh.

"Your chariot awaits you, princess." Cole smiles.

"Yes, thank you, mere peasant." As I turn to enter the car, I notice that the front of my car is lower. Looking downward, I realize that one of my tires is flat. "Are you kidding me?"

"Your tire is flat."

"Really? I wouldn't have figured that one out." I sarcastically commented.

"Do you have a spare? I'll change it for you."

"No, probably not. I've never had this problem before. My whole evening just got worse. First, the wild goose chase to find your friend, then you take me to your house to embarrass me in front of your parents, and now this.

"Embarrass you? What are you talking about?"

"I am a simple girl. Your parents will never accept me for what I am. Do you not see that?" I screamed.

Colton turns away and walks back to his car not saying a word. Realizing that I was too abrasive, I glance in his direction to make eye contact. He stares straight ahead. I hear the roar of his engine. Is he going to leave me here? I am upset about this stupid tire and taking it out on him.

Then I hear, "Are you coming or not, your choice."

"Forget it, I'll walk home." I lock my car door, slam it shut, and start walking through the parking lot. Cole slowly follows behind me for several feet then whirls past towards the highway.

I keep walking, focusing on the road before me. His tail lights disappear in the darkened landscape. I continue walking in attempts to keep my sanity. Do I call my mother to get me? I can see the gas station around the corner and that's where I am headed. I can have mom to pick me up there. She will be upset with me because she will have to bring Bekah with her. Tomorrow is her early shift as well. I can feel a "grounding" coming on. As I approach the storefront, I am startled by a loud, boisterous rumbling noise turning in behind me.

"Hey, girl. You need a ride?" a familiar voice asks.

I turn my head to see a large, red jeep. It was Nate.

"I am so glad to see you, Nate. Yes, I do need a ride home. Do you mind?"

"Get in here, girl. I'll take you wherever you want to go."

It is quite the challenge to climb into this lifted Jeep. Why a boy would want to sit so high in a ride, I'm not sure. My eyes are still scanning for Cole, but I do not see any sign of him.

"So, why are you walking out here tonight? I thought you were with Cole?"

"I was with him. We spent the evening together, he took me back to my car, I was mad when I saw it and made a rude comment and he left. My own stupidity. I deserved it."

"Let me guess, flat tire?"

"Yeah, how did you know?" I questioned.

"Lucky guess. It's not the first time he's taken someone back to their car and it had a flat tire. Jealous girls? I don't know. The whole point is that no one deserves to get left behind. Especially this time of the night. He will probably circle back around looking for you."

"I have to get home. I can't wait to see if he has second thoughts. Can you please take me home?"

"You got it, Chica." After several minutes the silence was broken, "What did you two do after you left the cave? Did he talk to you?"

"We went into town, followed two people in a tunnel, and then went to his house to meet his parents. We talked about sewer systems in the older homes, Sarah, that's about it."

"You can't leave me hanging, girl. You need to fill in the blanks. I'm all ears."

Realizing that Nate is one of the main leaders in this circle, I see no harm in telling him about our evening. Detail by detail, I give Nate all of the facts pertaining to our evening. He listens attentively while hanging on every word spoken. He doesn't speak, he only nods his head in agreement.

"Can I ask you something, Rachel?"

"Yes, you know you can."

"What do you see in Cole? His personality? His looks? What does he have?"

I was not expecting this interrogation. I look at Nate and question in my mind, why this is being brought to light? I know that he and I have some "tension" between us, but we do not have the same connection as I do with Cole.

"He treats me like a princess. He is kind, humorous, easy on the eyes, I don't know. Why are you asking?"

"Leaving you in the parking lot with a flat tire is treating you like a princess? It doesn't matter what comment you made. Is he truly kind or is that how it appears? Could it be an act? Just be careful. He is my friend and I adore him, but there has been some questionable occurrences that leave me guessing."

"Nate, I don't know what to think. The whole Sarah ordeal creates a sense of confusion. I don't understand how a family can give up so easy. And tonight, yes, I said something rude, but it is not like him to just leave."

"I will tell you this and if you tell Cole, I will deny it." Nate takes in a deep breath and pulls off the side of the road. At this point, I know that what I am about to hear will not be easy for him to explain. "The week that Sarah disappeared, Cole was acting strange. He was very distant and irritable. That's why so many people in the community were questioning his alibi."

"What? He didn't tell me that he was a suspect. Where was he when it happened?" I inquired.

"Of course he wouldn't tell you. He is representing himself as he sees fit to gain your approval. He is a player, Rachel. Can you not see through his deception?"

"I can't believe this. You cannot convince me that Cole is an immoral character. He has been honest with me about Sarah, the day of the disappearance, the items that were found. What else is there, Nate?"

"I should not be the one informing you of this, but it is evident to everyone that you are quite smitten by his charm. Open your eyes, Rachel."

"Nate, please tell me. I'm scared."

"Well, let's think about this. Have you ever wondered why the most popular boy in our school would be interested in you, the new girl? Why he had such an interest in you when you mentioned Sarah? Do you know something? I won't tell you not to hang out with him and I can't tell you who to fall in love with, but girl, you need to think about who you are dealing with." Nate explained.

"You're his friend? What's the difference?"

"I am his friend and always will be. Just because we are comrades doesn't mean that I cannot oppose his actions. Controversy. That's all I'm saying."

I feel overwhelmed with the whole conversation. Yes, I have wondered why he would be with me. We are from two different worlds. My lifestyle and his will never fuse without debate.

Nate continued, "The day before Sarah's disappearance, the whole gang set out for one of our cave explorations. When we were down inside the cave, Cole and Sarah were arguing about his parents and how she did not respect them as he expected. He said that he wanted her to leave. There was something mentioned about Sarah lying about the Lewis'. We all tried to ignore the confrontation, but we were spectators of the most dramatic performance of our lives."

"What happened, Nate?"

"Sarah left. I tried to stop her. She told me that she was going home. I offered to go with her, but she would have nothing of it. I lead her out of the cave and watched her drive away. I tried to follow her, but she was driving too fast. When I went by their home, she wasn't there. That's the last time I ever saw her. The next morning, she was gone." Nate's voice cracked and tears filled his eyes as he spoke the final words, "just please be careful."

"I will. I promise, Nate. I won't say anything to Cole." I reached over to touch his hand which was resting on the console. Nate looked at my hand and then to my face. With a disheartened voice he whispered, "Rachel, I'm scared for you."

Bright lights flashed from behind us making their presence known. We both whirl around to catch sight of our visitor.

"I would recognize those lights anywhere. There's Cole." Nate uttered.

We could hear a door slam and footsteps approaching the Jeep. I could see a figure marching forward in an impetuous manner; quick and with conviction. Nate and I immediately look at each other knowing that this situation could escalate with jealousy.

"Just stay in the Jeep." Nate ordered.

Cole stops at Nate's window and investigates the interior where we sit waiting for his vengeance. A look of resentment softens to one of relief when he realizes that I am beside Nate. He taps on Nate's window.

"There you are. I'm so sorry. I went back to the lot after I thought about everything you said and you were gone. I just started driving looking for you. When I saw Nate's Jeep, I was hoping that you were with him. Safe."

"I'm fine. Nate has offered to take me home. You don't need to apologize for leaving. I was disrespectful. I did not mean any of those things. I'll call you tomorrow, okay?"

"Aren't you coming with me, Rachel?" Cole questioned.

"Well, I just thought that if Nate didn't mind, that he could continue driving me home. No big deal, right?"

Cole starred at Nate scornfully. "Yeah, I would rather you ride with me, since your mother believes that you are in my company. Wouldn't that be wiser?" Cole strolls around to the back side of the Jeep to open my door.

"Probably," I unfasten my seatbelt, and lean over to kiss Nate on the cheek, "thanks for rescuing me. I owe you one." I turn to leave and Nate grabs my hand. Quickly I turn to face him. "What?"

"Call me tonight. I'll wait up." Nate pleaded.

Not wanting to make a scene, I nodded to approve.

"Let's go, Sunshine. Your mother is probably worried." Cole leads me to his car and we speed off into the night. Nate becomes a shadowy spectacle in my mirror.

Cole drives towards the other side of town not saying a word. The silence obliterates my sense of assurance. What if Nate was telling the truth? I need to form my own conclusion with every piece of evidence that I have been given.

"So, what did you and Nate do?"

"Nothing really. Just small talk. Why?"

"Just curious. I don't trust that boy with my girlfriend." Hearing him refer to me as his girlfriend brings a smile to my face.

"He is your friend. Why do you think he would do something inappropriate?"

"Nate has always been jealous of the things I have. He doesn't admit it, but I just know him that well. My family, our home, my car, and especially my girlfriends."

"I can't believe that. I am sure that he has no problems getting his own girlfriends. He's quite a charmer."

"He learns from the best." Cole says jeeringly. I punch him in the arm showing disapproval. "Every girl I have shown interest in, he immediately makes it a game to see if he can captivate them; control them. I find it entertaining."

"So, is that why you have shown interest in me? The simplistic, spunky new kid? Is this a game to you?" I questioned in a muffled tone.

"No! You are not a pawn in my game of life. What I feel for you is real. Are you not aware of the profound craving that I have for you? You are like air. I need you to survive. Not only do I need you, but I want you; every part of your being."

That was one of the most flattering statements that I believe my ears have ever perceived. I am entangled in his web of indulgence. Convincingly,

I possess enough courage to reveal my true feelings. I've never felt so strongly about someone else.

"Cole, without a doubt, you have given me a new outlook on life. I enjoy spending time with you. I'm just apprehensive about, well, what will happen."

"Happen, when? I would never hurt you, Rachel."

"Maybe not physically, but mentally you could destroy me."

"Never." Colton reaches for my hand laying on my knee. Gently he raises it to his lips, brushing the back of my hand, finally resting it on his cheek. In one sensuous movement, he glides my fingertips down the edge of his face and whispers, "You are so delicate. My only desire is to preserve your innocence; to protect you."

Caught up in the moment, I didn't realize that we had drove past my subdivision. Not wanting this moment to end, my mind and my heart begin to debate. Go home or face the wrath of Lyn in the morning? Exhausted from deliberation, I begrudgingly say, "Cole, we missed my turn."

"Oh, you can have your turn." he says with a huge smile.

"Too funny. We need to turn around and it's the second street on the right."

Whirling around in the middle of road, breaking the traffic laws, and showing no concern, Cole spins sharply into our neighborhood. I strain my eyes to see if the front porch light is on. Hopefully mom is in bed so she will not interrogate me about my evening. As we progress, I see the visible illumination. She's awake.

"Right here. This is my humble abode." I direct him into our driveway.

"Cute."

"Cute, that's encouraging."

"No, really. I think this is an adorable cottage. Small, but homey," Cole stops the car. "I would like to walk you to the door, if you would allow me to do so."

"My mom might be up. I'm not sure if you are ready for that."

"I love a challenge. Sit still, I'll come around to let you out." He says as he promptly arrives at my door.

"I could really get used to this."

"I want you to expect nothing less." Cole grabs my hand and leads me towards the front door.

"Oh, we always go to the side door. That's how I know that mom is awake. She leaves the front light on until she goes to bed. Habit."

"This place has a side door too?" he jokes.

"You know what they say, 'backdoor guests are best'."

"I find that statement disturbing and gross." Cole chimes in.

"Cole! That's not what I meant!"

The side door opens and there stands my mother. Dressed in her usual evening attire of fleece pajamas and fuzzy slippers, I cringe as I look at Cole. If only I could read his mind at this moment.

"Hey you! Glad you made it home safely."

"Hey, mom. Safe and sound."

"And your friend is . . ." my mother asked.

"Very pleased to finally meet you, mam. I am Colton Lewis. I sincerely apologize for our late arrival. There is a small issue with Rachel's car and we had a change of plans."

"What? Rachel, where is your car?" my mother, Lyn demanded.

"It's okay, mom. Just a flat tire. No big deal. I'll get it tomorrow."

"Okay. Remember that I have to go to work early in the morning. Bekah needs a ride to her friend's house around noon. I'll make plans for the garage to get it fixed by then." Lyn stated.

"I would love to stop by and pick you up, Rachel, and your sister. That way, there is no rush. It will be Saturday and garages can be overloaded. Of course, that is if it is okay with you, Ms. Collins." Colton, the charmer, added.

"I don't mind. I love seeing Rachel out of this house and enjoying time with her friends. What will you two be doing tomorrow?"

"Actually, my family is having a picnic down on the river lot and I would love for you and Rachel to come. After you close the shop, I would encourage you to join us. We have a cook out, sit by the fire, swim, tell lies," he winks at my mother.

"That sounds like a wonderful idea. Please, won't you come in? You don't have to stand outside." Lyn opens the door wide to allow entry.

"I appreciate the offer, mam, but I need to return home. My parents will be worried if I am out too late. I would like to continue our conversation at another time."

"Absolutely. Rachel, I'm going to bed. Turn off the lights when you come in. Very nice to meet you, Colton." Lyn responds as she withdraws into the house.

"Likewise. It is my pleasure, mam." Cole nods his head assertively. After mom disappears into the house, I step up on the stairs to attain eye level with my companion. Arms wrapped around my waist, Cole rests his head on my shoulder. I become aware of him smelling my hair. With each inhalation, I become stimulated. The heat from his breath on my neck, the stifled moaning divulging his satisfaction; I become entranced in the moment.

"Mom, Rachel's making out with some guy on the carport! That's disgusting!" Bekah screamed for all the neighbors to hear.

"Bekah, go back to bed! You'll wake up the neighbors!"

"So they can enjoy the show?", Bekah rolls her eyes and begins to inspect my boyfriend. From head to toe, she examines his clothes, his shoes, even his hair. I noticed her little nose in the air trying to capture his scent. "Well, at least you smell good."

"Well, thank you. You must be Bekah."

"And you must be someone that I don't know." Bekah taunts.

"Quick-witted. I like her". Cole looks at me and backs away. "My name is Cole. I'm your sister's new boyfriend."

"New boyfriend? ONLY boyfriend."

"Go back to bed, Bekah." I demanded.

"No, I'm having fun. You go to bed!" Bekah glares at me with both hands placed rigidly on her hips. An image of Ramona the Pest flashes before me.

"Cole, are you sure you want to take THIS in your car tomorrow? You can change your mind."

"Positive. She's adorable. We will be just fine. If she misbehaves, I'll duct tape her little trap and put her in the trunk." Cole cynically replies.

"Yeah, right. Your threats do not scare me." Bekah shifts her head side to side with lips pursed and one eyebrow raised. Pure attitude. She stands still waiting for a response. "You people bore me, I'm over it." She turns and saunters back through the house.

"I need to go. Thank you for an adventurous evening. I will see you in the morning?"

"I will be here around ten. Be prepared for more."

"More of what?"

"You'll see. Just be ready for anything. Casual dress and bikini." Cole said with an eager smile emerging without delay.

"Oh, I'm ready. I just hope you can control yourself when you see me."

"Let's hope not. Good night, Sunshine." He kisses my cheek and retreats to his car. I watch as he emerges onto the main highway and out of sight. The smile on my face dissipates as lights shine in my eyes from a vehicle parked in the drive across the street. Within seconds, I observe a large person approaching. I lean against the house trying to reach for the handle without taking my eyes from my intruder.

"Rachel, it's me."

"Nate? What are you doing here?" I said relieved.

"Do you think that I would just let him drive you home and I wouldn't make sure that you were okay?"

"How long have you been sitting there?" I questioned.

"Long enough to see you two enjoying each others company." he claimed obnoxiously.

"Stalker!" I jokingly noted.

"I'm not stalking. I'm protecting."

"All of this protection crap. You two are killing me. I'm home. I'm safe. Thank you for being concerned. I really need to go to bed, okay?"

"You know you can call me if you need to. I will always be there for you."

"Thanks, Nate. I appreciate that. I'll talk to you soon, okay?"

"Sure. Sleep well, girl." Nate waved at me as he traveled towards his Jeep.

"Hey, wait a minute." I called after him. "How did you know where I lived anyway?" I don't remember ever telling any of Cole's friends where I lived.

"I've been by here with Cole. He's had his eye on you for a while apparently. He just didn't bring you around us for some time after that. I guess after the farm incident, he decided to go public with it."

"He knew where I lived before I knew him that day?"

Nate did not respond. I don't know if its because he does not want to acknowledge my question or if he subconsciously accepts the fact that in my mind, Cole is virtuous and he is wrongly accusing him.

I enter the door and lock it behind me. Then, I check again before I head back to my bedroom. Before my head hit's the pillow, I'm fast asleep.

Tap, tap, tap . . . . tap, tap, tap . . .

I am awakened by a noise outside my window. As I leap from my bed to see who is there, I am surprised to see Cole. Standing there with his arms stretched out, he smiles at me and says, "Come on. Let's go for a ride."

"Are you crazy? What if my mom finds out?"

"I'll have you back before she turns over in her bed."

"Where are we going, Cole? I don't like surprises."

"You'll have to learn to love them. Come on!" he demanded.

Without hesitation, I ease myself on the ledge of the window as Cole guides my hips and places my feet on the ground. Complete darkness and silence surrounds us as we venture towards the road.

"Where did you park?"

"Right here. I couldn't take a chance on pulling into your driveway and waking your mother. I have plans for us."

"What time is it anyway?"

"Does it matter? Just relax and follow my lead." That wasn't the first time he has said that to me and each time I look at him bewildered.

"So, where are we going?"

"Stop with the questions before I get out my duct tape." He smiled, but after my conversation with Nate, I'm trembling inside.

"One more thing, Sunshine." Cole reaches into his pocket and pulls out a blindfold. "You need to wear this."

"You're kidding, right?"

"No, I'm serious." Cole opens my door, and places the blindfold around my eyes as I sit. "Can you see anything?" he asks.

"Nothing."

"Good."

His footsteps are heard coming around the side of the car, the door opens, and he fastens himself in. I become aware of him reaching around my shoulder and feel a strap across my chest. There is an audible "click" followed by, "Here we go."

We drive for several minutes, around turns and it seems up and down hills. It's hard to determine when you are unable to see, but that is what my mind is telling me. He has amplified the music to muffle the road noise or maybe the exterior world combined.

I notice that the car begins to decrease speed. That didn't take too long. This destination must be close to home. In my mind, I grow suspicious and theories of our whereabouts creates chaos beyond comprehension.

"We're here. Sit still for a moment. I will lead you."

As I sit patiently for him to free me from my restraints, I hear a distinct "thud" from the back of the car.

"Cole?" I said frightfully trying to break the silence. "Colton?" At this point, my inquisitiveness, along with my lack of self control, takes over and I remove the covering from my eyes. Outside I see nothing except murkiness and an occasional shadow from the clouds above. The full moon provides a dimly lit image before me. We are parked in a field. There are large trees along the edges, round bales of hay, and a small farmhouse, all contained within a broken, dilapidated white fence. I am familiar with these surroundings. I am convinced of that, but can not recollect how or why.

Slowly I emerge from the car. The brisk air takes my breath away as I am frantically searching to catch a glimpse of Cole. I inspect the area around the car and discover not one piece of evidence. Where did he go?

"Cole this isn't funny. Stop playing games!" I ordered.

"Rachel." a soft, sighing voice murmured.

"Cole is that you? Where are you?" I pleaded.

"Rachel."

Promptly I stride towards the location of the final whimpering. I observe something in the shadows beside a massive oak tree. Slumped over and motionless, I approach with caution.

"Cole is that you? Are you okay? Please answer me." I begged.

Shifting over on his side, Cole looks up at me. His eyes are covered with blood. Crimson red trickles from his forehead. As he tries to talk, blood spews from his lips and a shallow, gurgling noise comes forth.

"Cole, what happened to you? Cole, answer me!" Pure panic takes control of my body. Someone or something has mutilated my boyfriend and I will be next. I attempt to comfort him and brush the blood from his face while holding pressure on his wounds.

"Cole who did this? Where are they?" I peered deeply into his eyes to get a response. He focuses on my face, gives me a tender look, then abruptly stares fiercely above my shoulders. Mortal terror radiates threw my veins as I spin around to see my executioner. I will be next . . .

BBBBUUUUUZZZZZZZZZZZZZZZ . . . .

I am awakened by the sound of my alarm clock. My heart is still pounding loudly, my breathing is sporadic, my palms are sweaty; I have just lived through a nightmare. The image engraved in my mind is horrifying. A depiction of physical suffering, cruelty, and mutilation. I am troubled, however, due to the deprivation of knowing who was the assailant.

Nine o'clock.

"Bekah, get ready! Cole will be here soon." I walk down the hall towards Bekah's bedroom. She doesn't answer. "Bekah!"

"I'm in here. I've been ready. I'm watching TV while you're in there talking to yourself."

"Why didn't you wake me?"

"I thought you were talking to someone. I thought I heard another voice. I don't know. I don't care. I'm ready." Bekah turns and plops back on the couch.

I go back to my room to get dressed for the day. What should I wear? I pull out a variety of shorts, sun dresses, and rompers. After trying each outfit on and gazing hopelessly at myself in the mirror, I decide on a white sundress with eyelet lace and ornamental threadwork. This was a gift from my Aunt Aleigh. She is fashion chic, unlike those of us in this household. I slip on my white sandals and paint my toes a bright shade of pink.

"Okay. How do I look?" I asked my sister.

"Are you not going to shave those legs? That could hurt someone you know." Bekah smirked.

"Oh my gosh. I'm glad you reminded me. Yeah, I better take care of that before he comes." I rush into the bathroom and frantically engage in a leg-shaving frenzy. A few knicks and cuts later, I am done.

"Oh, she's in there shaving her nasty, hairy legs. I wouldn't go in there is I were you." Bekah exclaimed.

Petrified, I swing open the door to see my prince charming. Dressed in a polo shirt, khaki shorts, and flip flops he is the vision of manliness. Maybe modern "macho" male would be more appropriate. Dripping with lusty, unyielding power.

"Are you ready, Sunshine?"

"You bet I am!" I taunted him by flipping my hair towards his face and swirling my dress. His expression was priceless. Visible torture.

"Absolutely stunning. Let's go before I get into trouble."

"What are you two doing? Making out again?" Bekah asked.

"No, we were planning our day. Get your things, let's go, kiddo."

"Whatever." Eyes rolling again. "Natalie is at her house. Can we go now? I hate waiting." Bekah groaned.

"We are right behind you." Cole said. As we follow Bekah out the door, we are deafened by her ear piercing squeal.

"Are you kidding me? We get to ride in that?" Jumping up and down and running to Cole's car, she is the exact representation of a lively, vivacious child.

"I get shotgun."

"I don't think so, Bekah. Climb in the back."

"You are so jaded." Bekah remarked.

"Bekah, how about I come over one day and take you on a ride, just me and you. We can get ice cream or something." Cole replied.

"Sounds good to me." Bekah flashed me her 'I always get my way' look.

We drove into town, past the courthouse, the movie theatre, the bakery, and into the Graham Addition. There were lovely homes located on these streets. Larger than ours but not as impressive as the Lewis'. Children riding their bikes on the sidewalk, parents raking freshly cut grass, everyone up bright and early to start the weekend.

"There, the brown house. That's Natalie's."

"Natalie . . . McClung?"

"Yeah, how do you know that?"

"Brandon McClung. He has a younger sister and this is his house. He calls her "peanut" so I never knew what her name was. Guess it's Natalie."

"There she is. Pull in slow so she sees me in this thing." Bekah says as she leans between the front seats to make herself more visible. A freckled face, red-haired girl runs up to the car laughing.

"Is that your car, Bekah?" Natalie asked.

"No, it's my friend, Cole's, he drives me around. Like it?" Bekah turned to give Cole a wink to seal the deal.

"Do I? That's hot. He's hot too!" Two giggling girls run to the front porch and wave.

"I'll be back tomorrow to pick you up, okay, Bekah?" Cole stated.

"That would be cool. See you later!" The friends disappeared into the house.

We pulled from the driveway and traveled into downtown. Shoppers were scurrying from store to store in their weekend rush. Unique shops filled with every goodie imaginable. Pricey, but a good variety of merchandise. The coffee shop stands before us with its aroma seeping from the pores of its percolators.

"Hey, can we stop for a minute to see mom?"

"Of course. I would love to see mom this morning." Cole flashes his pearly whites. Meticulously, he parks the car directly in front of the shop. All eyes are on us. I feel like I'm the star of a theatre production. As he opens my door, he reaches behind me and grabs my butt.

"What are you doing?"

"Giving them a show. They were expecting something, you were wanting something, it's a win-win situation."

"How do you know that I want something?"

"Girl, you are all but obvious." Cole smirked. "I'm joking. I was trying to get you to breath. Relax. Quit worrying about what other people think."

He's right. We walk through the door and approach the counter. The smell of freshly brewed coffee consumes the room. The jangle of beans in the grinder resounds in the air. Unusually crowded today. Mornings are busy, but there is an overabundance of people here.

"Hey mom. How's it going?"

"Great. Busy, busy. And you guys? Headed to the river?"

"Yes, mam. Please remember that you have an open invitation to join us. I promise that you will enjoy yourself."

"I just might do that. It depends on how tired I am after slaving here all day. You guys have a fantastic time. Enjoy the day!" mom gleamed. We turned to leave the room when mom called for us. She looked bewildered. "Rachel, remember that photo that I had hanging in the back hallway by the storage area?"

"Which one?"

"The one with the people standing by the entrance of the shop. Remember, the people that used to own this building?"

"No, I'm sorry, not really. Do you need me to help you find it?"

"No. I'll keep looking. I just don't understand where it could be? It was there the other day." Mom whirled around to take a customer's order. "Oh, and Cole . . ."

"Yes, mam?"

"You touch my daughter inappropriately; I will rip your arm off and beat you with it." Lyn stated matter of factly with a smirk.

"Yes, mam. I would like to keep my arms." Cole replied.

"Get out of here. Have her home by eleven, in case I don't talk to you all later."

"Yes, mam." Cole grabs my hand and we swiftly leave through the front door. Back in the car our conversation starts with the mystery. A missing picture from my mother's shop wall.

"Do you remember seeing it the other night, Cole?"

"No, but to be honest, I was not looking at the walls. I don't know why anyone would want a picture of some previous store owners. Probably some kid playing a prank."

"I guess you're right. I wonder who the previous owners were?" I questioned.

"I'm sure they are not here, so why concern yourself?"

We continue traveling down Route 60 to the bottom of the hill. Veering left, we drive alongside the river on a narrow country road. I gaze out my window, watching people float downstream on rafts tugging their beer raft behind them. There are also fisherman perched on the banks trying not to look so obvious as they stare at the young ladies basking in the sun.

"Our place is here on the left." Cole acknowledged.

"This is beautiful. I've never actually been down to the river. It looks so peaceful."

"We enjoy coming here in the summer. We have a small camp right on the edge of the river. Nothing fancy." He says as we turn into a narrow, wooded drive with a gate.

"Nothing fancy, huh? The gates? Are they for security?"

"No, just for looks." he laughs.

Through a tunnel created by overhanging tree branches, we slowly come out at the other side. In our sight is a cedar-sided home which is on stilts. The lawn is well manicured with an abundance of flowering trees and bushes.

"I guess your gardener works here as well?" I joked.

"You are such a smart ass."

From the deck we see faces appear. His parents, the Longs, and two others that I have not had the opportunity to meet. All dressed as if they were off to brunch at the Greenbrier, tidy and meticulous.

"There you are! We were wondering if you would make it for brunch. Nancy will have it ready in a few. Come on up." Mrs. Lewis shouted.

"Sorry, she occasionally gets a little like trailer trash. Hand her a beer and a cigarette and there you have it."

"Again, your humor is killing me." I commented.

"Oh, yeah, before we go, I have something for you." Cole reaches under his seat and pulls out a silver package wrapped with a delicate pink bow. "I know that pink is your favorite color and the silver is just 'blingy'."

"You didn't need to get me anything."

"I know that I didn't need to, but I wanted to. Open it."

I carefully pull back the edges one at a time with great precision. I remove the tape slowly not to tear the shiny silver covering.

"Good grief, it will be dinner time soon at this rate. Rip the thing!" Cole slings my hand away and starts shredding the paper into tiny pieces.

"Okay, okay. Let me do it." I begin to speed up the process. There was another box inside which had a note taped to the lid. It read 'For your next adventure'. When I pried off the lid, there was a brand new camera. Much nicer than the one that I crushed under the farmhouse. This one had an expensive, attachable zoom lens and leather carrying case. He even had it monogrammed with my initials.

"Cole. This is beautiful. How did you remember?"

"I remember more than you realize. I wanted to get you something that you would enjoy on our adventures together. No more trips alone, right?"

"No, I believe that I had enough of those. One and done."

"Come on, let's go in before my mother sends security out." We walk from the car and up the flight of stairs onto the massive wooden deck. Hanging baskets of flowering plants adorn the rails surrounding the perimeter. There is an abundance of windows and French doors around the entire house. Every room has its own spectacular view of the Greenbrier River.

"Wait here. I have something special planned." Cole strolls inside and returns moments later with a picnic basket, blanket and smile on his face.

"What is this?" I pleasantly asked.

"There is nothing more romantic than a picnic lunch by the river. I asked Nancy to prepare a little something for us. She's the greatest!"

I must be the luckiest girl in the world. I have met the most genuine person. His sincerity and humbleness captivates me. How could I ever have doubted him? And the dream, so real, that was my sign that Colton is not the villain. How could I be so mislead? The dream. The farmhouse. It is all coming back now. I had been there before. That is the old Persinger Farm where Cole rescued me. The first time we met. Why did I not realize that sooner? My thoughts waver as I try to recollect the events that evening.

"How is this? Does it meet your approval?" Cole lays down the blanket and looks at me for confirmation.

"Lovely. The water gurgling, the frogs croaking, birds chirping, this is the most relaxing environment. I am amazed at its beauty and tranquility." I lay down on the blanket and stare peacefully into the trees above us. Cole finds his place beside me. He places his arm behind my neck and I turn to rest my head on his shoulder. "I am amazed by you." I softly whispered.

I drift off to sleep for several minutes until I am startled by someone screaming and a loud splashing noise coming from behind me. I spin around to see a rope dangling from a tree limb and Cole splashing around like a kid in a new pool.

"Come on in. The water feels great!"

"How long have I been asleep?"

"I don't know. An hour maybe. You looked so peaceful that I couldn't wake you . . . until now. Come on."

"But my suit, I need to change." I shuddered.

"I'll turn my head. Go behind that big tree over there."

"But, what if someone sees me?"

"Who? The fish? A bird? We own this whole section of the river. Our closest neighbor is miles away."

"But what if someone floats by?"

"They won't. Our section of the river is from the northern forks and it is blocked so that no one can pass through. Will you come on?"

Begrudgingly, I tiptoe across the soft green grass and find a place behind the large tree to undress. I peek around the edge to make sure that Cole is still in the water and not looking in my direction. I remove my panties and slip on the bikini bottoms. I place the strings around my neck and tie them as I slide the sundress over my hips and to the ground. Reaching around the back, I fasten my hook to hold everything in place. Slowly, I creep around the trunk of the tree towards the rivers edge. I feel the smooth pebbles beneath my feet and the sand squishes between my freshly painted toe nails. The water is inviting, but not as enticing as my boyfriend. He lifts his pointer finger giving me the 'come hither' gesture. Step by step, I move closer to him not knowing what to expect. I hope he doesn't submerge me in this water.

"Wow. YOU look amazing. I didn't realize how shapely and impressive you were underneath your clothes. You have well defined muscle tone. Why do you hide behind layers of cloth?"

"I am a runner. That's what I did at my last school. I didn't join here because, well, we usually do not stay long enough for it to be worth it." My fingertips grazed across the surface of the water as I spoke.

"I'm in awe." Cole steps towards me and reaches with his hand beneath the water. I feel his finger skim along my outer thigh and continuing to my lower back. He grasps firmly and forcefully jerks my body against his. The water creates a wave as our bodies become one in the water. His arms tightly embracing my back, he lowers himself to sit on the river bottom. I wrap my legs around his waist and brace myself against his chest. As we sit in the river, he sweeps the hair back from my face as his tongue brushes against my lower neck. His smooth and skillful movements, are the result of a mastered technique that are beyond the years of adolescence. I move my head allowing him to feast upon the sweetness of my neck. With one experienced snap of the wrist, I could feel my bikini top loosen. Grabbing my chest and falling backwards, I get a mouthful of algae and fish poop.

"That was not nice." I scorned holding my chest with the bikini straps entangled within my fingers.

"It was a joke. I closed my eyes just like this." He demonstrates by tightly squeezing both eyes closed then peeking through one of them.

"Fasten me back, please." I turned from him to allow direct access to buckle the strap.

"Hold still. You have to move your arms. Can you hold up your hair please?" Cole instructed. As I lifted my hair from my shoulders, I could feel his lips pressing against my spine. He softly licked my shoulders and kissed my neck. Again, I was in his trance. My body began to tingle all the way to my toes. It was a sensation unlike no other. I could feel him fondling the strings of my bathing suit. He was trying to figure out which loop to insert the plastic hook. Boys . . . .

At once, his weight shifted and he slid backwards. My top flew threw the air like a football looking for the receiver, out in the open, for all to see. It landed approximately twenty feet from us and continued to float downstream.

"Colton Lewis! My top! Quick get it!" I screamed.

Cole tried to capture the top but was not a match for the swift current.

"Now what?" I asked sternly.

"I guess you will have to go topless out of the water. That is such a shame." Cole snickered.

"Oh really? Well, I guess you won't need these!" I sprinted onto the bank, holding my chest while grabbing his dry clothes. I held them over the water teasing him.

"You wouldn't dare."

"Oh, wouldn't I?" I threw his shirt into the water. "Oops." I playfully taunted.

Cole inched closer as he picked his shirt from the water.

"You don't need these." As I was preparing to drop his shorts, he leaped from the water's edge and tackled me in the grass. We started laughing. He tightly pressed his chest against mine so that my skin would not be exposed.

"Persistence . . . ." Cole turned his head and handed me my sundress.

As we start back, Mrs. Lewis frantically yells for Cole to hurry up. We run towards the house to find his mother slumped over in a chair hysterically crying. Her hands are shaking as she tries to reach for us.

"Mom, what's wrong?" Cole requested.

"Nana has had a heart attack. She is not doing well. We have to leave tonight for Tampa." she said sternly.

"Is she at the hospital?" Cole asks.

"Yes, and has apparently been admitted to the Intensive Care Unit. I'm so sorry that it happened today. I know that you wanted everything to be perfect." Emily continues to cry uncontrollably.

"Emily, that's your mother and we need to be there with her. I'll call the airport and have the jet fueled and ready for us within the hour. Let's go home and pack. We could be there for a while." Looking in my direction, Dylan continues, "I'm sure that Rachel understands."

"Absolutely. You need to be there. Cole, can you just drop me off at the shop and I'll catch a ride home with mom after work." I smiled politely.

"Shouldn't I stay here to take care of the house?" Cole's concern diverted.

"The house will be fine. Nancy has the codes and will keep everything in order. There is no need for worrying. We need to focus on Nana right now." Dylan commanded.

"You're right, dad. I just need some things taken to school on Monday and . . .", Cole started to say.

"I'll take them for you. No big deal." I interrupted. I look towards the door and motion for him to follow. I need to convince him that it would be best for him to go. A few days apart might make him miss me. We stand on the deck, gazing across the river, and listening to mother nature.

"You realize that you need to be there, not only for your grandmother, but your own mother."

"I know, but we could be gone for a week or so."

"And your point is?" I sarcastically jeered.

"My point is that I don't want to be away from you that long" We begin walking towards the car.

"You're right. You might plunge into a condition of extreme desperation and hopelessness." I smirked.

"Yeah, or you might fall aimlessly in love with my best friend Nate." Colton poked me in the ribs.

"Get over yourself. Take me to the shop before you instigate an argument." My point was proven. Cole opened my door and kissed me on the cheek.

He whispers under his breath, "I know that you are smarter than that." I pretend that I didn't hear his comment. Once again, we are driving towards town. Looking at Cole, I observe his expression of concern. A look of worry and anxiety flows from his pores. Deep in thought.

Suddenly, he jerks the car to the side of the road, "I almost forgot." Cole reaches into his pocket and pulls out a pink box. "I got you one more thing. I wanted to give this to you tonight, but since our plans have changed, there is no time like the present. Get it, present?" he laughs at his attempt of humor.

"How can you change your emotions so quickly?"

"What are you talking about?"

"I don't know." I look down at the box, "You really should not buy me gifts. I appreciate them, but it is not expected."

"I saw this and thought of you. I want you to wear it." Cole stated proudly.

As I lifted the lid, there was a beautiful, shiny, silver locket. In the shape of a heart, it opens into two halves. On one side, there is a miniature picture of Cole. It is the same picture that I saw in his bathroom the other night. I can see the torn edges where the picture was separated. The other side has a few tiny scratches. I imagine he tried to slip in a picture of me and changed his mind.

"This is beautiful!" I exclaimed, "I love this picture of you. Where is the rest of it?" I taunted.

"Not there anymore. That's an old picture, but I have fond memories."

Wonderful. Fond memories with a stunning brunette. Every time I wear this, I will speculate about her and their fond memories.

"That's nice." All sincerity has rescinded.

He holds both ends of the necklace, "Turn around. Let me put it on you."

I lift my hair and swivel in my seat. His hands cross in front of me then brings the chain to my neckline. The cold metal feels refreshing against my skin. For a moment, I quiver. "That looks ah-maz-ing on you, princess." Cole's eyes light up as he admires his gift.

"Thank you, Cole. You really know how to make someone feel special."

"Girl, you haven't seen nothing yet." he winks.

Back on the road, we progress up the hill towards town. On the right, Cole's house sits solitary. Trees, of every shape and size, line the perimeter along with a brick barrier. I can see the gated entrance. In the darkened night, I was oblivious to the unforeseen beauty of this fortress. A large white iron gate stretches across the drive and above it the word "Tranquility" appears.

"Do you need to stop to get your things for school?" I asked.

"No, I'll drop them by your house, if that's okay with you?"

"That's fine. I'll be home later this evening, just leave it on the porch if I'm not there."

We descend into town and come to a stop in front of the shop. Colton looks bewildered.

"Call me tomorrow after you settle in. I'll miss you." I said pouting.

"Ditto." He leaned over and placed his lips gently against mine. "Please stay out of trouble." His fingers linger in my hair and down to rest on my thigh.

"I will do my best."

Cole climbs out to open my door. I watch him in the mirror. Pure ecstasy. His powerful stride with his muscular chest distended with confidence. He glides along the side of the car and stands on the sidewalk peering through my window. Perplexed by his lack of progress, I hesitate. Anticipating some form of amusement at my expense, I decide to let myself out. Standing face to face, our bodies inches apart, I ask "What are you doing? Why didn't you open my door?" I argued.

"I was just pondering what it would be like to have no arms." Cole looks over my shoulder and wiggles his fingers towards the shop window.

As I turn around, I can see my mother looking in our direction. She smiles and waves back shaking her head.

"You never stop, do you?"

"I don't think you will complain." he says as he leans in for another kiss. He moves my hair behind my ear and whispers, "You'll be begging for me to stop."

"If mom doesn't rip off your arm, I think she should rip off another appendage."

Smugly, Cole replies, "I could do the cougar thing", as he raises his hands to display a playful, clawing motion.

"Get out of here! Call me later." I turn to cross the street and see my mother standing at the window. Before entering the door, I hear "Bye, Ms. Collins! I like these!" Cole begins waving both arms wildly to provoke my mom.

"He is insane, Rachel. Absolutely hilarious." my mother says.

"Yeah, he's something alright."

"Why are you back so early?"

"His grandmother is in the hospital and they are flying to Florida today."

"Oh, how sad", mom's eyes focus on the locket, "and he gave that to you?"

"Yes, isn't it beautiful. Look inside." I pry open the hinges to display the photo inside.

"Very nice. Now, you'll need one of yourself. I'm sure you have several at home. You're always getting photos for Facebook and your phone is a collage of, well, you."

"You act like I'm vain." I argued. "I'm not vain, I am just self-aware."

"Meaning . . . you are aware of yourself?" mom joked.

"Exactly." I stopped to look around the shop. "You're going to be here for a while. Do you need help or should I call someone to come get me?"

"To be honest, I have a date this evening and have made plans for Louella to finish my shift tonight. Bekah is at her friend's and I thought you would be entertained. It's still early, I can cancel."

"Cancel? Are you crazy? Have fun and I'll call Lindsey to see what she has planned for the evening." I spin around to gather my things and then tenaciously begin my cross examination. "So, who is this complete stranger?"

"He is not a stranger to me. We talk frequently."

"And his name is?"

"None of your business." mom replied.

"Witty. Well, I need a name in case you show up dead tomorrow in a ditch. A name would be nice."

"Wesley Painter. Happy?"

"Very. He's that pro golfer from the club, isn't he?"

"Yes, he is."

"The Italian with the dark hair, muscular physique, dark skin, gorgeous brown eyes. You go, mom!" I raised my hand to give her a high five. She must not be feeling the love. She only shakes her head.

"How do you know so much about him, Rachel?"

"Well, when you had a sudden interest in the game of golf, I knew there was a reason. So, one day I went there investigating and asking about lessons; there he was. Very pleasant. I bet he is the romantic type with candles, wine, evening strolls . . ."

"With my luck, it's Tiger Woods on the Wii and a Corona." We both giggle like school girls. "Don't wait up for me. You'll be fine by yourself, right? He mentioned staying at the Greenbrier."

"Go girl, get it, get it!" I started chanting.

"Rachel!" Mom was trying to act mad in her own disturbingly, non-violent way. I believe she has spanked me once in my life and I cannot recollect Bekah receiving even one. That's probably what's wrong with us. We are craving discipline. NOT!!

I retreat to the back of the shop to call Lindsey. On the second ring, she answers.

"Hey, Lindsey, it's Rachel . . . . what are you doing tonight? . . . really? I'd love to . . . I'm at the coffee shop . . . Nate? . . . oh, that's fine. I'll wait for him here . . . Great! . . . . Bye!"

"Plans?" my mom asked.

"Yeah, Lindsey is sending Nate to pick me up and I'm going to her house to hang out. I might just stay the night. That's okay, right?"

"Sure, be careful."

Time passes slowly as I wait for Nate. I pace back and forth by the front window watching cars pass by. There is a crowd of customers flowing through the entrance to get their evening java fix before they watch a performance at the Greenbrier Theatre. A live performance with actors and actresses from around the world and locally, who provide us with an hour or two of their lives to entertain ours. The last time I was there, it was The Greenbrier Ghost series. I was so fascinated with the story that I asked mom to drive me to the final resting place of the main character, Zona, out at Sam Black. Her gravestone diminishing from years of deterioration. What a sad ending to a sad life.

"Do you need a ride, chica?" a deep voice yelled.

"Nate!" I ran to the side of his Jeep and heaved myself into the front seat. With the top down, this will be an interesting ride. Air whipping hair in my face as we rumble down the road, I can feel the vibration from the engine under my feet. I lean my head back on the headrest to look into the sky above us admiring the formations of the clouds. Free, spirited, weightless. That's how I feel at the moment. I grab the dash and stand to my feet leaning towards the windshield arms outstretched.

"Are you having a Titanic moment?" Nate laughs.

"This is so exhilarating! I love this feeling of rebellion."

"What?" Nate asks.

"Going topless with the wind in my hair, rumbling of the motor, I feel like a rebel."

"Yeah, that's how I like my girlies, topless and loud." Nate gave me a wink and maintained his course. "Going to Lindsey's for the night?"

"Yeah. I don't want to be alone tonight. I had a terrible dream last night."

"What happened?"

"Cole drove me to the old farmhouse, he was mutilated, and the killer was going to kill me when I woke up."

"The farmhouse where you were found? Who was the killer?"

"Yeah, Persinger Farm. I didn't get to see their face. It just freaked me out."

"Have you been back to the farm since the incident, Rachel?"

"No, I'm terrified. Not of the farmhouse, but of the reason I could have been there. I don't remember anything."

"Why don't I go with you? You know that I will not let anything happen to you."

"But, what about Lindsey? Look at my dress. White. Really? I'm not dressed to climb around in the basement of an old house."

"Behind my seat is a bag of clothes. I have some sweatpants and a sweatshirt that you can wear. Don't make excuses."

"But Lindsey? I want her to come too."

"She can come along. It will be fun. Better than sitting around watching movies. Besides, maybe if you return, your memory will also."

"She is expecting me."

"She'll be fine. I was going over to help her with homework, that's why she asked me to stop on the way to get you. I'll call her and tell her to meet us there."

"Does she know where it is?"

"All of the kids in Lewisburg know where the Persinger Farm is. It's one of the notorious, most haunted places in town."

"No, you're lying."

"I would not lie to you." Nate said with conviction.

After several moments of convincing Lindsey to risk her life at the farm, Nate was able to finalize the details. Lindsey would meet us there in the field and the three of us would all gather at the farmhouse gate. As we approached the gravel road, I could see the structure on the horizon. Everything was as I remembered from my dream. The trees, the rolls of hay, the fence, exact duplicate copy.

"There's Lindsey's car parked by the pond." Nate noted.

"I'm glad she came along. It doesn't look obvious."

"Obvious in the fact that you want to find a reason to get me in another dark, secluded place? Girl, stop begging." Nate proclaimed.

"What is wrong with you boys. Always a sexual deviation of facts. Yes, it will be dark, yes we will be alone, but if you think for one second that I would beg you for anything, you are sadly mistaken."

"Touche."

Springing from the Jeep like a cat on crack, Nate races across the field and over the time-worn, wooden footbridge with his caving back pack in hand. "Let's go girlies. The three Stooges, the three amigos, great things happen in groups of three."

"Like the Father, the Son, and the Holy ghost . . . you'll meet them soon if you don't watch yourself." I yelled.

The house that once stood proudly on the hillside, guarding over it's golden fields of hay, now fallen shambles of brick and shattered wood. Carefully we climb over remnants of years gone by. It is essential that we move forward with great caution. My rescuers were trained professionals and we are like CSI "want to be's". Our investigation team would consist of Lindsey the Whiner, Nate the Nonconformist, and Rachel the Indecisive.

We gradually reach the ledge where the squad had to lift me over when I was beneath the earth. Laying on our stomachs, we hang our heads over the side to get a closer look. It smells of musky, moldy, dirt and worms.

"This is disgusting guys. I can't go down there. It is so nasty." Lindsey complained. I didn't give her the title for nothing.

"Lindsey, it's the same as the caves. Dark, damp, stinky. What's wrong, Barbie? Ken's not here to protect you?"

Lindsey flashed him a look that would send him somewhere with explicit directions. She glances at me which creates a feeling of uneasiness.

"Nate, you go down first and tell us what you see." I ordered.

"No problem, ladies. I am all about making both of you happy, preferably at the same time." Nate grinned.

"Go, Nate. Do you need a drum roll?" I smirked.

"No, professionals do this for pure gratification, amateurs need the attention to build up the nerve." Nate leaps from the ledge into the darkness. After several minutes of bumping around in the dark, we hear, "Looks good, ladies. Nice flat area. It appears to be the basement. There was a set of stairs to my left, but when the walls crumbled, it has blocked the area. It's muddy, but doesn't look too dangerous. Come on down."

"Rachel, I can't do this. I will wait for you two at my car, okay?"

"Really? Well, don't leave me here alone with him. Cole will flip."

"I wouldn't do that. I'll be right outside, in my nice, clean, fresh car."

Taking a few steps forward, I realize that it is my turn to descend into the pit. I try to focus my eyes into the darkness to catch a glimpse of my companion.

"Nate? You ready?"

"Always. I'll get your legs. Just lay on your stomach and slide down."

Following his directions, I lay down with my legs dangling over the edge. The temperature difference is evident even with Nate's bulky clothes. Feeling myself lowering into the hole, I notice that there is one hand on my right butt cheek and another hand on the back of my left thigh.

"Nate, I'm trying to stay focused. You need to remove your hands from my bottom."

"Well, I could but you'd fall. I'm not grabbing your butt, I'm stabilizing your weight."

"You are so full of shit!"

Nate bursts into laughter. His melodramatic comments create an emotional reaction of pleasure. I am drawn to him, but not the same as Cole. I feel a sense of security and commitment with one and the other, I feel an erotic, lustful appetite for danger.

"Well, let's do it." Nate slings his back pack on the ground and removes two flashlights and his "trusty" notebook.

"Are you sure about this, Nate?"

Nate stands before me with a blank expression on his face.

"Do you trust me, Rachel?"

"Yes, of course I do. Why do you say that?"

"We will not do anything that you do not want to do." Nate says as he winks.

That's what I'm afraid of. I want to do a lot of things with him. I must stay focused and not on his masculine physique.

"Let's do it." I agreed.

"I knew you wanted me." Nate gloats as he prances in front of me.

We use the flashlights to inspect our surroundings. I cringe as I scan this large, open space that we have become part of. What once was a floor is now layers of mud and fallen leaves. There are spider webs attached to the walls; swaying from side to side with drifts of air. The exposed, rotted wood shines with years of algae and slime. The putrid smell of decay permeates our clothes.

"Do you hear that, Nate?" My eyes turn to scrutinize the area under what once were steps leading to the floor above. As we move closer, we see something emerging from the home's foundation.

"What is that? It sounds like wind blowing." Nate says.

"Under the house? That doesn't make sense." I look at Nate with displeasure. We both approach skeptically as the whirling resounds before us. There against the wall is a hatchway.

"A door? Are you kidding me? There is another floor?" I peered at Nate with dismay.

"This has to be the basement. They couldn't have dug through all of this rock. Maybe a side cellar, but not another level." Nate studies the door to find the handle. Only slabs of wood.

"This looks familiar." Nate chuckles to himself. "Roll up your sleeves. Let's open this Bit . . . thing." He catches himself mid sentence. "You grab that side and I've got this one." We both jerk and strain trying to separate this boarded plank from the existing structure. Or at least, what's left of it.

"What's that?" I point to a small wooden board protruding from the side of the wall and laid across the bottom of the door.

"Really?" Nate says sarcastically as he slides the board back allowing the door to open. "After all of that and we just needed to move a board." Nate says shaking his head.

"What do you see, Nate?

"Stairs. There are man-made wooden steps leading downward. We have to go."

"Let's tell Lindsey what we're doing. One of us could get hurt, you know."

"Good idea," Nate pulls his phone from his pocket, "I'll call her." Several seconds pass, no answer. "Stay still. I'm going up to tell her myself." He emerges from the rugged cavity.

Solitary, I become an observer of the dilapidated ruins of a family's existence. Why would I be here? Gazing around to reorganize my thoughts; tranquility evades my soul. A sense of fearlessness and courage erupts from within. Surprisingly, I do not fear the one that I am in search of or is in search of me. I embrace the spirit of Sarah.

"Sarah, are you here?" I whisper. "Please let me know if you can hear me." Discouraged; I walk towards the ledge where Nate ascended to wait for his return.

"Be Careful."a voice whispers.

I whirl around towards the utterance. "Be Careful? Why? Am I in danger here?" My eyes scan the room, blinking, trying to focus on my companion.

"Him."As this word is spoken, a chill from the passageway thrusts into my chest.

"That hurt. You don't have to do that to get my attention. What do you want me to do?" I feel pressure on my spine that forces my body towards the wooden gate. "You want me to go in there?" The door opens.

"Rachel? Where are you going?" Nate screamed.

"I was just looking."

"You need to freakin' listen. I told you to stay still."

"What is your problem? Why are you so mad at me?"

"Sorry. It's not you. I went up to tell Lindsey that we were going down the stairs and she's not there."

"What? She said she would stay."Adrenaline flows rapidly through my veins. Why would she leave?

"We're okay. I've got my cell phone if we need it." Nate steps closer, "If you want to leave, tell me now before we go in."

"I need answers Nate. You are the one that can help me." In more ways than one, but I will not tell him that. Conflict within myself of choosing between Cole and Nate. It's an ongoing battle.

"I am here to please. I guess our threesome has now become a pair. Besides, I don't think you'd want to share me with anyone." Nate humors himself. "Great things come in pairs too. For a girl, you've got a nice pair. And me, representing the guys, I've got the biggest around," Nate says as he turns his back, bending slightly while fumbling with something before him. I here a zipper opening. "Wait until you see my pair of . . ."

"Nate!"

"What?"

"I don't want to see them!"

Nate faces me once again. Holding two pairs of caving shoes that he apparently retrieved from his backpack. I exhale and laugh cynically appreciating his humor.

"Shoes? Look at these shoes," Nate strolls over to stand beside me, his mouth inches from my ear, and provokes me by saying, "Girl, you couldn't handle the other set." Nate grabs my hand, pulling it towards his waist, "You better stick to these." My new pair of boots. The look on his face. He is so proud of himself.

We start our journey down into the darkness. Our flashlights reveal an endless flight of stairs extending well beneath the Earth. This is not a cellar; it's a tunnel or passageway.

"I'm confused. We need to document everything. We don't want to get lost in here. We also need to take mental notes of everything that we see before us." Nate explains.

"Oh, I am." I was aroused by the view in front of me. Hormones . . .

"I just counted step number twenty and we are still not to the bottom."

"Yes, I agree." I had no clue what step we were on, nor do I care. He has now crossed over to his "spelunking" mode. "Nate, where is the wind coming from?" I asked as a breeze blew through my hair. "It's not chilly in here as it was in the cave."

"Perplexing. It does not have the characteristics of a typical cave either. I believe it's a passageway. Do you see those?"Nate directs my attention to small lanterns affixed to the wall.

"Lights?" I questioned.

"Yeah, that's odd."Nate stated. "Old mining lamps. Maybe this is a mining camp. Wonder if we'll find something rare and priceless?"

We continue through the burrow, ducking occasionally to maneuver within the fabricated underground passageway. I speculate that we have now crossed at least seventy steps when we approach a small nook to the left side of us. We both look at each other knowing what the other is thinking. Simultaneously, we trudge forward. We enter the vault with caution, not wanting to provoke an unexpected guest. Inside, there are minuscule piles of rock debris, grayish brown in color, with large slabs of what appears to be limestone placed on top of each creating seats. Four assembled structures still emerging from the earth, the others have crumbled from years of subterranean existence. On the chamber walls, chiseled numbers and names emerge as we approach with adequate illumination.

"Lewis 1842," I begin to read each section individually, "McClung 1844, Morgan 1867, Johnson 1910, Evans 1913," bewildered, I continue to pivot as my eyes frantically scrutinize every name that appears, "Forde 1920, Collirs 1935." I cannot comprehend what my eyes are reading. As I turn towards Nate, his face reveals the pain from centuries of deception.

"So, is this why you all have formed this little clique?" I questioned. "Every one of you are represented on this wall." Sarcastically I add, "Is this part of the town's secret society?"

"It all makes sense now." Nate whispered, "We were all part of his game."

"What are you talking about, Nate" I ask in dismay.

Hands thrown in the air, pointing at the walls as he spoke sternly, "Years ago when Cole formed this caving group, I didn't understand his selection of people. There was a history between the Lewis' and the McClung's, everyone is aware of that. Why was there such an effort to become friends? Cole and I were the only ones who were true friends. The others were arranged by him." Nate turns away from me, "I am so freakin' stupid. He played us all."

I placed my hand on his shoulder in hopes to comfort him, "Nate, I don't believe that it is a game. Maybe it is God's display of forgiveness; letting the families know that the past is the past."

"And maybe you are too naive. Can you not see through his illusion of trickery, princess?", Nate comments, "Did you not see your name?", Nate turns to point at the wall, "Read it again."

"Collirs 1935." I specified.

Nate approached the wall candidly, wiped his hand across the surface, placed the flashlight against the wall, and said, "Try again."

Before my eyes were the letters C-O-L-L-I-N-S. Astonished; I sat on the cold, man-made rock seat to allow my mind to contemplate what my eyes have perceived.

"But why? I don't understand."

"I don't think we are meant to understand. We are just to play along." Nate said as he started out of the nook entrance. "Let's keep moving. I've documented and charted. Nothing else here for us." Nate replied, "Nothing at all."

We walked in silence as we navigated deeper into the tunnel. Neither of us uttering a word. Pebbles beneath our feet cracked and crumbled with each footstep. There is an evident temperature change in our surroundings, but oddly it's not colder. I want to question Nate about it, but for someone who has so much to say, he is torturing me.

"Nate, there. Do you see that opening ahead of us?"

"Yeah, why?"

"I think I remember standing there. I was looking for someone."

"Who?"

"I'm not sure. I can't think. My mind is so overwhelmed at the moment. So much to think about. Cole and you, you and me, and . . ."

"Why don't we sit down and relax for a moment and then we'll start again. We have all evening, so there is no need to hurry." Nate comforted me.

His voice was like a soothing melody to my ears. His sweet, tender tone reassuring with each distinctive word. His eyes widen and glisten as he looks at me. We are in a section of the passage that resembles a short wall emerging from the earth and behind is the actual brown clay reaching towards the ceiling.

Nate sat on the edge of the wall and motioned for me to sit in front of him. He spread his legs open to allow room for me to fit between. I follow directions well. In a smooth, gentle motion, Nate begins massaging my shoulders. The tension within my body fades with each stroke. He rubs from my shoulders to the center of my back and down below my hairline. His fingers wrap around my ribs as he holds his thumbs tightly against my lower back. My mind wanders as I feel the warmth of Nate's body pressed against mine. As he gently caressed my skin, it tingled with anticipation. The seduction begins as my breathing deepens . . . .

Feeling as if my attraction for Nate will overcome my love for Cole, I hastily say, "I can't do this, Nate."

"What? Enjoy a massage? I'm trying to get you relaxed so you can remember. Let me help you."

"But, I don't want us to . . ."

"To what? Nothing will happen between us. You have made your decision. Trust me, will you?" he scorned.

"I'm sorry."

Nate commences to his prior duties. I realize that Nate is harmless. I need to be more concerned about myself. I am the one in control of the situation. He is being a gentleman and I am looking at him like a cupcake at a weight watcher meeting. I need an intervention.

"Relax. Try to remember the day."

I close my eyes and reminisce. I concentrate on my breathing. Slow and deep. I concentrate on my surroundings, the breeze in my hair, the familiar scent of clay, the trickling of water from the ceiling, I concentrate on Sarah.

"Nate, I remember that I was taking pictures here. Of the pond and the fields. There was a girl at the house. I came here to follow her. She lead me into this tunnel, but she disappeared. I never found her. I blacked out. Somehow they found me under the house. My mom said a girl named "Sarah" called her. It doesn't make sense."

"What did she look like? Do you remember?" Nate asked.

"I vaguely saw her. Brown hair, maybe? I can't say for certain. I did take a picture of her."

"And where is it?"

"Destroyed. My camera was destroyed."

"Why would someone bring you in here? We need to see where it leads. That's the answer to the mystery."

Nate continued to rub my shoulders and moved towards my neck. Abruptly, he stops. He turns my shoulders around to face him and forcefully grabs the locket in the palm of his hand.

"Where did you get this?" he snarled.

"Cole. He gave it to me."

Nate inspected the locket carefully.

"Where did he get it?"

"I don't know. He didn't say. Why are you so interested in this necklace? It's no big deal, Nate."

"You're probably right. I'm just overprotective."

"I think that's sweet."

"No, it's not." Nate looks down at his hands and then back to me. His piercing blue eyes demand my complete attention.

"What, Nate?"

"I can't lie to you. Rachel, I have strong feelings for you. I know that you are in love with Cole and I would never do anything to destroy your happiness, but I must be true to myself and let you know how I feel. The chemistry between us when we were in the cave together. Passion. Did you feel it too?"

"Yes, but Cole . . ."

"I know. I understand. I will wait for you. I will protect you as long as I can."

"What are you talking about?"

"I've told you. Something just isn't right with the stories. Cole is not as innocent as you believe. He can't be. No one is that perfect. His family; their money."

"Are you jealous?" As soon as those words entered the air, I wanted to take them back.

"Jealous? Of what? He has nothing I want other than you."

"I don't know what to say?"

"Nothing. Just be my friend."

"You know I'm your friend and I will not tell Cole about this conversation. I won't tell him about being in the cave alone with you either."

"Yeah, that would be an interesting conversation." Nate laughed. "Let's keep moving."

Time passes quickly as we venture through the tunnel, winding and turning, up hills and down, mapping our journey for documentation. I know we have lost track of time and we have been beneath the earth for quite some time, but we must keep marching forward. This is my time to find answers.

In the distance, I see a break in the wall. It appears to lighten in color. No longer the red clay, and sand, but becoming a gravel mixture and the walls widen. Our feet shuffle as we stroll up to the corridor. We quicken our step as we become eager to see what lies before us. Have we reached the end of the our tunnel?

"Nate . . . ." As I look before me, I am speechless. My heart drops to my feet and I stop breathing momentarily. I cannot comprehend what is before me and how it is possible. After walking miles beneath the existence of Lewisburg, the hustle and bustle of everyday life, we are now faced with this. Our course has intertwined with the tunnel system under downtown Lewisburg. "I can't believe this."

"What?"

"We are downtown."

"What! That's impossible." Nate said.

"No, really. This section goes towards the bank and this one the court house."

Nate looks in each direction, puzzled, and says, "You are serious, aren't you? How do you know this?"

"Yes. Very serious. I've definitely been here before," I look to the left towards the direction of the bank, "Well, Cole and I have been here before"

"Who has access?"

"Some shops have doors. Did you not know?"

"I've heard things, but didn't believe it. It's hard to imagine people moving slaves, money, and bodies."

"Bodies? What?"

"It's no secret. There was a huge rivalry between the Lewis' and the McClungs'. Rumor has it that one of the Lewis gang was murdered and the body was moved in a tunnel beneath the town. The body disappeared. Vanished."

"Brandon McClung's family?" I questioned.

"Yeah. Crazy isn't it? The descendants of generations past become best friends years later. I guess blood isn't as thick as they claim it to be," Nate shakes his head and continues, "Wait, you and Cole were down here together?"

"Yeah, long story," Nate gave me his continue with the story look, "We followed Kamryn and Tristan into her dad's shop. Well, apparently I followed them and Cole came in after me", I had to stop to catch my breath, "There was a doorway in the storage room that led into the tunnel, we followed the footprints leading into my mother's shop, went inside, didn't see anyone, and left." That was exhausting.

"Well, we are at a point in our lives where we must make a choice. Do we take this road to the left", Nate points in the direction of the bank which is a well worn path, "or do we take the road to the right which has been less traveled?" Nate points to the right towards the Court house. "Funny, this makes me think of the similarities between Cole and I, with myself being the less traveled, innocent angel of course."Nate winks in response.

"Oh, and Cole is well traveled, or experienced, I should say?"

"Your typical, charming jet-setter." Nate looks down, sighing, revealing a poor attempt of acting skills.

"Bravo." I clap my hands to reward his performance, or lack of, "To the right it is. I need the less traveled, slower pace," I look with desire into Nate's eyes, "Do you think you can help me with that?"

Nate nods in approval. He grabs my hand and leads us to our destination. My legs ache, my head is throbbing, but my heart is saying to stay on course. I am starting to doubt Cole and his sincerity while I am realizing the gentleness and honesty of my Nate.We are unprepared for the road less traveled. Hidden from the light of day, this path passes along side the stream beneath the city. The water, rippling across rocks and sediment, flows swiftly. It simply appears from the wall. The stories are true, there it is before us, the underground stream.

"This stream must come from the top of the hill, towards the post office. Cole's parents were talking to the Long's about the stream under the homes being used for septic disposal." I snarled my nose at the thought of poop floating beside us.

"Well, you know, they say that their shit doesn't stink." Nate added, "for once, I agree with them. I can't smell anything." We both laughed.

The walls started looking more characteristic of the cavern we explored. The tunnel became more narrow, the clay walls filled with jagged rock formations, the drop in temperature; we were transcending into a cave. As we passed through several chambers, the unexplored pit before us, our stamina was depleted.

"Can we stop now?" I asked.

"I think that's a good idea. We've been gone for a while." Nate opens his backpack and spreads a fleece blanket on the clay earth, "I don't want you to be dirty." Nate lays on the cloth and pats the space before him. "I promise to behave. Lay here so we can stay warm while we rest." Nate pointed to my arm, "Set your watch alarm, don't forget. We'll just rest for about an hour."

"Promise to be a man of your word? You'll keep your hands to yourself?"

"I promise." Nate held out his pinky to perform the swear ceremony. We link fingers and giggle.

Carefully, I lay in front of Nate. He curls himself tightly behind me. His arms surround me. His head is tucked against my shoulder. Our breathing becomes rhythmic. My mind searches endlessly for reasons as my heart memorizes what I am feeling at this moment. My friend, my Nate, my Hero. I become drowsy. I fight the urge to close my eyes, but become victim to a deliberate slumber. Intentionally, the alarm is not set. I might be Rachel the Indecisive, but as my mother says, Rachel the Self-Aware. I am aware of myself liking two boys at the same time . . . .

I awaken embraced within Nate's arms. I don't think we've moved.

"Nate," I patted his arm, "Nate, wake up." I turn to face him. He must have lit a candle beside us, the wax melting onto the rock as it creates a dim illumination around us. His angelic face shines in the flickering candlelight. I fight the urge to touch is face, but cannot resist. Gently I caress his face with my fingertips, slowly along his cheek, and across his lips. Fascinated with his masculine features, I find myself captivated by his beauty. I raise my head, and gently kiss his plump lips. The warmth of his lips against mine, the entanglement of our bodies, I become engulfed with satisfaction. Such a delectable buffet of manliness and I am hungry! My body tingles with sensations that I have felt with Cole, but more intense. Unable to control myself, I decide to crawl on top of his chest to lay on his body.

As I move, Nate peeks from one eye saying, "Well, that took you long enough."

Nate presses against my body, lowering me against the ground. Eagerly, he passionately begins to kiss me. He does so with such intensity. Every movement of his tongue is so calculating and precise. He does know what to do to make my body tremble with anticipation. It is completely mental at this point. Nothing physical. He has complete control of my mind; my psyche.

"So beautiful," He pulls his head away and brushes my hair away from my face. "He does not appreciate you the way I do." At that moment, he convinces me of Cole's lack of gratitude.

"I don't know what to do, Nate."

"Just follow your heart." Nate kisses my forehead, "I'll wait for you to decide." He looks down at my watch, "Oh, no. You didn't set your alarm!"

"So, we've only been asleep for a little while."

"A little while? Try all night!", he flips my wrist around and I see 5:35am in bold, bright, red numbers.

"We need to go, I need to get to Lindsey's!" Hurriedly, we begin tossing our belongings back in the bag and blow out the candle. "The candle was a nice touch." I proclaimed.

"What? Not mine." Nate stated matter of factly, "It's not yours?"

Suspiciously, I glance around the room, "No," my eyes quickly scan for anything else out of character, "We weren't alone, I guess, but who? Lindsey? Maybe she came in to check on us."

"Lindsey is scared of her own shadow. She would not come all the way in here looking for us," Nate's eyes widen, "When was Colton leaving?"

"Yesterday afternoon. He was going to drop something off to my house on the way out of town. I don't know when he'll be back."

"Okay, good. Well, no one is here now, they didn't hurt us, so they must be our friend." Nate placed his hand on my shoulder guiding me from our midnight slumber spot.

Feeling an uneasy sense of being stalked by a predator, we sprint all the way back. It is fortunate for us that we are both athletic and natural runners. The trek from beneath the earth was like a cross country meet on a massive overload of steroids. Up hills, jumping rocks, diving under crevices, down hills, leaping three wooden steps simultaneously, splashing through puddles, all the way to the crumbled ruins of the Homeplace.

Our efforts were rewarded with the morning light awakening our senses as we emerge from the darkened pit. The golden hay sparkles with dew drops as the sun glows bright in the sky. A freakish pink-yellow hue.

"No sign of Lindsey or anyone else for that matter. We're safe." Nate tosses his bag in the back seat and steps aside to allow me to climb in the Jeep. He braces my lower back with one hand and holds my other in his. As I turn to sit, he lifts my hand to kiss the back of it. "I may not be as romantic as Cole, but I will show you that I care." I smile showing approval.

Growling of the engine and rumbling of huge tires against the cold pavement, we travel directly to Lindsey's house hoping to reach our destination before she and her family awaken from their beds. No lights are visible from the end of their long driveway lined with plum trees.

"Here, let me out here." I motioned for Nate to stop, "You'll wake them if you drive closer. I will tap on her window. She'll let me in."

"Go check and I'll wait. Just signal from around the house, okay?" Nate said.

I ran up the driveway and around the backside of the house to Lindsey's bedroom window. There sitting on a block with his arms crossed, enraged with anger, was my boyfriend, Cole. I stopped abruptly in my tracks.

"Where have you been?" Cole grumbled.

"I thought you were going to Florida?" I delayed.

"And so you felt the need to stay the night with another person?" Cole's eyes squinted as he faced me in the sunlight. I could see that he had been crying. "How could you do this to me?" Feeling worthless, I can't look him in the eyes. "I didn't do anything wrong."

"You didn't?" His eyes pierce through me, "I don't believe you. Who were you with? Do I even need to guess?"

Hearing footsteps racing in our direction, I whirl around to stop Nate from encountering a confrontation. The shadow emerging from around the corner didn't resemble a familiar figure.

"Well, look what we have here," Brandon sarcastically comments, "When the cat's away, the mice will play."

"Brandon? What are you doing here?" I asked stepping closer to Cole.

"I'm here with my FRIEND, your EX boyfriend." Brandon exclaimed.

I turned abruptly towards Cole hearing that comment to see his response. "Ex boyfriend? Are you kidding me?"

"Rachel, where are you?" There is the familiar voice I need to hear.

"Nate, stay back. I'm okay." I begged.

"Oh, so this is who you were with? Nate? My best friend." Cole shook his head, "You bitch," he looks to the corner of the house, "Hey, Nate, come join the party!" Cole shouted as he pinned my arms behind me and pressed me against the house.

Brandon positioned himself against the side of the house in a crouch like position ready to pounce on his prey. His eyes focused on the galloping shadow as it floated closer.

"Nate, go away! They will . . ." I tried to speak as Cole grabbed my mouth tightly.

"You need to hush,angel", Cole gnarled through his teeth as he thrust his body forcefully against mine, "You've caused enough trouble."

As Nate turned the corner, Brandon leaped from his hiding spot and knocked him to the ground. Punching, kicking, spinning in all directions, arms flailing around, clothes ripping; two wild animals attacking each other.

"Stop it, Nate! Let him go or I'll hurt her!" Cole yelled.

Nate immediately released his rival from his grasp. Brandon sucker punched him in the stomach to show his appreciation. Nate bent over spitting crimson red from his mouth and fell to the ground riving in pain. "What is wrong," Nate spits, "with you guys?"

A chill runs down my spine and I faintly hear someone say "Get him out of here, they'll kill him." I look around, but there is nothing. Cole doesn't even hear the voice. He just continues his interrogation.

"What's wrong? You spend the night with her and then you expect me to accept that?" Cole demanded. "You know how much she means to me!" He loosens his grip on my arms. I break away to stoop beside Nate. I take off my jacket to place it firmly against his mouth to stop the bleeding.

"Colton Lewis, you've lost your mind!" Realizing that things have worsened quicker than I thought, I must think fast, "I went to the cave yesterday by myself, Nate found out and came looking for me. If he wouldn't have shown up, I'd still be down there . . . lost." I look at Nate to let him know to follow my lead this time. "That's all. Nothing happened." I step towards our accuser. "Why are you so mad?"

"So, you two didn't plan this?" Cole simmered.

"Cole, I would never hurt you." I walked towards him again.

"Candle light? Ask her about the candle lit room, Cole?" Brandon blurted.

My head whipped around to face the nark. Brandon knew about the candle. He was the one with us.

"You had candles?" Cole interjected. "I thought this wasn't planned?"

"You knew about that, Brandon? That was nice of you to have those ready for us." I said smuggly.

"What? Tyler told me that you all were in there all night and had the candle lit. All snuggled and romantic." Brandon said.

Tyler, the brother, should have known. Lindsey must have told him we were there. He is one of Cole's soldiers. He must have placed the candle there last night. How did he find us?

"I couldn't walk any further and we decided to take a break. Yes, we laid on a blanket together to stay warm. Yes, we were exhausted and apparently fell asleep. No, WE did not light a candle nor did we plan it to be romantic. Get over yourself, Cole." I turned to look back towards Nate, "Thank you, Nate, for helping me last night."

Cole looked like a scorned child, "I guess I overreacted. I went by your house to drop off the homework, you weren't there, and when I called your mom, she said that you were at Lindsey's. Tyler tells me that you are with Nate . . . I shouldn't have jumped to conclusions." He turns to Nate, "I'm sorry, man. I know that you would never do that to me. Are we good?" Cole extends his hand to help him to his feet.

Nate grabs his hand and rises to his feet, "Yeah, man, we're good." He briefly pauses as he looks in my direction, "You know what they say, 'bros before hoes'." Nate winks.

"Ha ha! Now that I've watched 'Bi Polar Express', I'd like to get some rest." I yawned.

"Let me take you home, Sunshine. You need to be in your own bed." Cole held my hand to lead me to his car.

"What about Lindsey? She's probably worried."

"No, Lindsey is fine. We talked last night." Cole looks towards Lindsey's window. My eyes follow his. "She's good," he says reassuring me, "She's real good." he whispers. For a brief moment, I could have sworn that I could see her curtain move. As if, someone was watching.

Nate steps away from the others and starts towards his Jeep, "Rachel, I've got some of your things in the Jeep, let's get them, okay?"

"Sure." I agreed as I smiled at Cole, "I'll be right back." Promptly, I join Nate around the side of the house. As we traipse down the driveway, Nate grabs my arm forcefully. The look in his eyes is frightening.

"You are coming with me."

"What?" I said in disbelief, "Nate, you have to get out of here. They will hurt you if they think that something is going on between us." I begged.

"I don't care about me. I am concerned about you." Nate urged as he quickened our pace. "You have no idea what you're messing with."

"Nate, he said everything is good. I need to stay with him so that he will not get any crazy ideas."

"Crazy ideas like what?", Nate turned to face me, "Like the fact that you and I have chemistry between us? That I like you and you feel the same way? That when you kissed me, for that one special moment, he was the furthest thing from your mind? Please, Rachel, tell me some of your crazy ideas."

Realizing that the jokester Nate that everyone knows and loves has a very sensitive side as well, I am speechless. Truth. He is speaking the truth.

"You will think I'm crazy, but when you first came around the house, I heard a voice that told me to get you out of here or they would kill you." I place my hand on my forehead as I turn to face him, "What the hell is going on, Nate? There was no one standing near me. Have I lost MY mind?"

Nate exhaled loudly and surrendered. With certainty, as we stood there face to face, Nate faced a revelation, "Sarah," he continued," Sarah was my girlfriend."

"What! Why are you telling me this now?" I shoved him backwards, "You knew that I needed answers."

"You needed answers?" Nate scorns, "My girlfriend simply disappears from the face of the Earth and no one cares! Let's put this into perspective." Nate continues.

"Is that why you went with me, to see if she would appear?"

"Yes." Nate shamefully admitted, "In my own sadistic way, I thought that since she is drawn to you, I would be able to feel her presence. I miss her pureness; my delicate rose.", Nate takes off his jacket, pulls up his sleeve and reveals a tattoo wrapped completely around his bicep. Pale green vines, tiny leaves, and prickly briers intertwined artistically, "all I'm left with are the thorns." As I take a closer look, I can visualize the name Sarah within the vine.

"That's amazing. I didn't notice that before."

"I created this myself. A tribute to Sarah. It reminds me that I must never stop looking for answers."

"And the kiss? That wasn't real was it? You were trying to upset her?" I said as I looked to the ground in shame.

"No, that was real." Nate lifted my chin, "I can't chase ghosts forever. It would be nice to have someone to love again."

A chuckle echoes from a distance as clapping commences. "Bravo! Bravo!" We hear. "Nate, the lies need to stop. Did you tell her that you were the last one to see Sarah alive? Did you tell her about the argument you had?", Cole approaches, "Rachel, did he tell you that Sarah broke up with him the day she disappeared?" Feeling deceived, I turn to face Nate as I step away, "No, I didn't think he would. If anyone is guilty of murder, the cards are stacked against you, Buddy. My parents and I have looked the other way because we believe everyone deserves a second chance. There is no hard evidence to say that you killed her, but you are the one with the motive, not us." Cole strolls closer and places his hand on Nate's shoulder, "Just let this go. You and I have come to terms with this before. Forgive and forget, remember?"

Rejected, Nate turns away and continues to his Jeep. As he starts out of the driveway, his eyes filled with tears subconsciously admitting defeat; he has confirmed my worst fears. Maybe Colton is right. Maybe Nate has been deceiving me the whole time. Keep your friends close and your enemies closer. Nate would benefit the most from my knowledge of Sarah, right?

"When will you ever learn to trust me, Rachel? I am only trying to protect you." Cole sighed.

"You want to protect me, Nate wants to protect me, who's next?" I murmured.

"Nate? He needs to protect you from himself," he added, "That boy has issues. Sarah saw through him eventually. He was a stalker. He would just appear for no reason."

The whole time Cole is talking, I can understand the similarities. The night my tire was flat, showing up at my house unexpectedly, going into the cave with me and Lindsey, and so on. Am I his next victim?

"Cole, just take me home. I can't deal with this right now."

"Let me get Brandon, he will have to come with us." Cole added as he disappeared around the house.

My cell phone begins to vibrate in my pocket. As I take it out, I see a new text message from Lindsey. It reads "Why did u tell me 2 leave yesterday? Now u r n my yard?"

I text back, "u left first."

Lindsey replies, "Nate said u wanted me 2 leave."

"When?" I sent.

"When u were in the pit"

"Call me, Lindsey." I typed frantically.

Her response, "Gotta go".

Now it makes sense. Lindsey didn't leave on her own. Nate went up and told her to leave us there alone. He had everything planned knowing that precious Lindsey would not go into the pit. Two pairs of boots, not three. I'm not a gambling person, but I want to see Nate's call log. I bet he didn't even dial Lindsey's cell phone either. I am such a fool!

My phone vibrates again. This time it is from Nate. I am so distraught that I contemplate not opening the message, but my curiosity takes over.

"I am sorry for hurting you. You wont see me again" the message read. Discouraging, oppressive words from a broken spirit. Feeling as if everyone is against him. I don't know who to believe. My response to back to him,

Nothing.

Cole and I drive off towards my home after taking Brandon home. I stare blankly out my window consumed by thoughts of Nate. I cannot comprehend the turmoil he is experiencing. Does he feel that I hate him? Does he feel like everyone is against him?

As we approach my neighborhood, I notice a police car parked in my driveway. There is a police officer standing at the front door talking to my mother. Immediately, I know that I am in trouble. I did not call mom and she must have come home early.

"Cole, I am in big trouble."

"What? Why?" he asked.

"I thought mom would be gone and I didn't call last night. I fell asleep." I continue to observe them on the porch trying to read their facial expressions.

"I spoke to your mom last night. She was fine." Cole smiles to put my mind at ease. Pulling into the driveway, mom looks at me. No, she stares through me. I jump from the car and run to engage myself in their discussion.

"Mom, what's going on?" I questioned.

"Rachel, this is Deputy Dave Roman. He is looking for a Nathaniel Evans?" Lyn paused looking at the filth on my clothes, "Your friend, Lindsey, said he was with you last night." Lyn peered at me with one brow raised.

"Yeah, he was." I stated as I look at Cole solemnly. "We were just with him, at Lindsey's house. He should be home soon, sir."

"I will notify his parents. You all have a good day." Deputy Roman turned away, then faced us again, "Can I ask where you were last night with Nate Evans?"

Begrudgingly, I respond, "At the Persinger Farm."

"The abandoned house? That's trespassing, young lady. Let's not do that again." Deputy Roman nods as he tips his hat and returns to his patrol car. I watch him pull away from our sight.

"Well, you have a lot of explaining to do," mom started interrogating, "why in the hell did you return to that farm? I thought we had an understanding. You were not to go back there."

"Mom, I am searching for answers. Who was the girl I was following? Where is Sarah's body?"

"What! I thought Sarah was a student from school?", mom's voice converted to her demon tone, "You lied to me? Wait . . . her body?"

It was a lie. I had told so many lies to conceal the facts that at this point, I don't even know the truth. "Mom, Sarah was Cole's sister. She is dead, I think. I don't know anymore."

"Ms. Collins, mam, let me try to explain." he strolls toward my mother, "Sarah disappeared about a year ago. Her body has never been discovered, only a few bones and some of her clothing. My family lost hope some time ago."

"Then who was the Sarah that called me the day Rachel was found?" Lyn inquired.

"That's the mystery. To our knowledge, Sarah is dead. She has to be, but someone must have been playing a joke or just ironically chose a name that has linked our lives together." Cole fondly adds, "Whatever the case may be, I have been truly blessed with your daughter's friendship."

"Whatever the case may be," mom smiled, "thank you for bringing her home safely. Rachel, you need to get some rest. Colton, we hope you will visit us again soon." Lyn gracefully entered the home.

"I am tired, Cole. Will you call me later?" I asked.

"Absolutely." He kisses my forehead, "Sleep well, Sunshine."

I lay on my bed, collecting my thoughts, and trying the decipher the information. Images of the day flash before my eyes. I drift away . . .

"Rachel! You need to get in here now!" Lyn screams from the kitchen.

I turn my head and land in a puddle of drool on my pillow. Cold, saturated, white cushion. I must have been more exhausted than I thought. The clock on the wall says eight thirty and it is getting dark outside. I stumble to the door and creep down the hall to face the Queen of our castle.

"Yeah, mom." I casually say, "What's up?"

Mom steps from the door and I see my new best friend, Deputy Roman. Nonchalantly, he makes his entrance.

"Good evening, Rachel." He began the conversation, "May I ask you a few questions?" Deputy Roman challenged.

"Yes, sir," I walked over to the kitchen table. This could take a while, "What's wrong?"

"Nate Evans has not returned home today as you anticipated." Deputy Roman pulls out a small notebook and pen from his jacket, "Do you have any idea where he might be?"

"Me? No." Shaking my head, "Why would I know? Have you checked with his group of friends?" I said.

"Are you not his girlfriend? His parents said that you were in a relationship. Nate also told them that the two of you were going on a camping trip together last night." Deputy Roman looks up from his notes, "So, you were the last one to see him, I presume."

"I last saw Nate leaving Lindsey Morgan's house when Cole brought me home. Nate is not my boyfriend." I tried to observe his notes, "Have you talked to Cole? To Lindsey?" I blurted.

"I have attempted to reach Lindsey Morgan. Her brother, Tyler, told me that she went to stay at a friend's house, a Sarah McClung. As for Colton Lewis, his family will not allow me to talk to him without a lawyer present. That's what all rich people do." he advised.

"Deputy Roman, we might not be rich, but I am intelligent enough to realize that you are suspecting that my daughter has something to do with Nate's whereabouts and since she has given you her side of the story, I believe that this conversation is over." Lyn walks towards the door, opening it slightly, "If you have any evidence against my daughter, you may return, if not, I never want to see you on my premises again. Good day, sir." The door is opened wide and Lyn motions with her arm the direction she wishes for him to follow. Out.

"I appreciate your time and I apologize if you felt as though I was interrogating your daughter. Please call the department if you hear from him." He hands me his card, "I'm just trying to find the boy."

"Yes, sir. I will." I take the card from his hand and lay it on the counter. He exits our home.

"What is going on, Rachel? You better start talking now!" Anger lingers in her voice.

"Sarah McClung? Don't you get it mom? Tyler made up the name. There is no Sarah McClung. That's Nate's last name and Cole's missing sister's first name. This is a game to them! Maybe this is a code. Maybe they are trying to lead me somewhere?"

"Rachel," Mom drops her head to scrutinize, "First, you are chasing ghosts in abandoned houses and now your friends are using codes so you will play Nancy Drew. What are you doing?"

"Mom, I am as confused as you are. I need to find Nate or Cole and get to the bottom of this chaos. Can I use your car?"

"Mine? Use your own." she added.

"Mine has the flat tire, remember? Did you have it fixed?"

"No, not me. But it's parked in the side yard." she said puzzled.

I grabbed my keys and ran outside. There it was, in all of its glory. I opened the door and jumped inside. As I give the car the once over, I notice a tiny piece of paper placed under my windshield wiper. I roll down the window and open it quickly.

It reads: Call me A.S.A.P.

LM

Immediately, I dial Lindsey's cell phone. She picks up on the second ring.

"Lindsey, what's going on?"

"Rachel, you need to get over here. Something is terribly wrong. Nate is missing! Police have been here, they've seen his blood in my yard, your jacket, please come get me. We need to find him."

"Where? Where would he go? I pleaded.

"If I had to guess, he would go to the only place he feels safe. The caves." Lindsey stated.

"Or the tunnel."

"What?"

"The old house. There is a tunnel leading to town. He would possibly go there." I directed, "It's not as cold, nor is it as damp."

"I'll meet you there in ten minutes, okay?"

"I'll be there, Lindsey. Be careful."

With urgency, I rapidly flee from the house and travel to the farm. The moonlight provides a path for me to follow through the darkness. Narrow, curvy roads with no street lights or guardrails. Tonight is the exact replica of my nightmare. The smell in the air, the temperature, my stomach churns as I approach the farm entrance. I know how this night ends, but only with one difference. Cole is not present. Lindsey has not arrived yet, so I decide to park by the remnants of the home and wait.

My phone vibrates in my pocket. It's Colton.

"Hey, Cole."

"Where are you?" he questions.

"Just hanging out. You?" I respond.

"I'm just heading home. I've been hanging out with Brandon."

"When did you and Brandon become such good friends?"

"We've always been friends. I've just spent so much time with Nate that he felt neglected."

"Speaking of Nate, have you seen him, Cole?"

"No, I can't say that I have. He's probably just hiding out somewhere trying to get your attention, Rachel."

"My attention? Cole, that's ridiculous." I bite my lip as I try to remain calm. He cannot find out about me and Nate.

"Think what you will, but that boy has a crush on you. He'll turn up in a few days. When he thinks it's not working, he will come out of hiding."

"I hope so. I feel bad for him."

"Nate's a big boy, Rachel. He'll be fine. He's just hanging out somewhere."

"You're right." Seeing Lindsey's lights shining over the hill, I realize that I must get off the phone, "I'm so tired, Cole. I'll talk to you tomorrow, okay?"

"Sleep well, Sunshine. Good night."

"Good night." As I hung up the phone, I put down my window to greet Lindsey. As the car pulled closer, I could see that it wasn't Lindsey, but Tyler. He stepped from her car and started towards mine.

"What are you doing, Tyler? Where's Lindsey?"

"She's at home. I saw everything that happened this morning." he said.

"That was you at the curtain?"

"Yeah, it was me."

"So, you wanted a front row seat to the production you created?" I sarcastically added.

"What?"

"Brandon told us that YOU told him about us being in the tunnel. Did you set the candle too or was that Brandon? You two amaze me with all the games." I step from my car, "So, again, where's Lindsey? She called me to meet her here."

"That wasn't her. That was me."

"No, clearly it was Lindsey's voice."

"Yeah, I told her to call and what to say. You need to figure out the good guys and the bad guys, girl." Tyler walks to meet me, "I did not tell Brandon anything. I heard him say that this morning. He was calling your bluff. And Lindsey, she wants to be with Colton. Have you not picked up on that?"

"I've heard the snide remarks, but didn't feel it was something to be upset about." I look Tyler intensely in the eyes, "and you, how do you fit into this scenario?"

"I am Nate's true friend. I'm not pretending like most of the others." Tyler looks at his feet, "I want to find my friend and I thought you might be able to help. The cops were there today. They saw blood and you left your soaked jacket."

Listening to his testimony, I am overwhelmed with emotions. "So, what's your plan?"

"Rachel, I've tried to call him all day. He is not answering. His crazy ass always answers. After watching the show this morning, I know that something has happened to him."

"You expect me to go into the tunnel with you."

"I was hoping for that, yes." Tyler pleaded.

I gazed into the pit. Darkness. "Let's go. We won't find him out here. Hopefully he's cooking us dinner and will serve it by candle light." We both laugh.

Tyler, being the tall, dark, and handsome preppy boy, actually looks stunning in his jeans, boots, and Izod fleece pullover. It's important that we look our best when we are faced with death. Not being as physically fit in stature, climbing into the pit is more difficult with "Dapper Dan". I will have to carry him most of the way. Dangling over the edge, we lower ourselves with a "thud" as we hit the floor beneath us. As I stand, I notice that Tyler has already started opening the wooden door under the stairs.

"How did you know that the door was there?" I huffed.

"All of us know about this place, Rachel. This was one of our big hangouts when we first got our driver's license. No one would come here looking for us. It's haunted, you know."

"Yeah, so I've heard. Have you been through the tunnel?"

"Of course. Colton would take us on tours to his house for fun. We'd hang out for a while then we'd stop by the McClung's bakery for dessert, the Forde's for coffee, and back to the farm." Tyler's chest puffed out as he spoke being so proud of his adventures, "All in a night's work."

"The Forde's owned a coffee shop?" I questioned.

"Your mom's shop. You didn't know that?" Tyler lowered his brows gesturing disbelief.

"No, I didn't." We started walking down the flight of many stairs, "This tunnel leads to Cole's house?"

"There is a secret door behind the mantle in the library. We would sneak in and out all the time. His parents had no clue we were gone."

"That's very interesting." Picking up the pace, I am aware of the time frame that we are dealt. We need to search quickly for Nate. "So, will Lindsey tell Cole you are with me looking for Nate?"

"No need to worry about that. I have her cell phone, our home phone is unplugged and hidden. Besides, she is tied to her bedpost." Tyler giggled.

"What? Where are your parents?"

"They went out of town tonight with friends. I told her if she behaved I'd let her go tomorrow. Sibling rivalry." We both laugh.

Deeper and deeper into the tunnel we trudge. No sign of Nate or a struggle. I take Tyler to our sleeping spot, but he isn't there. We venture towards the downtown shops, but no footprints are present.

"Do you feel lucky, Tyler?"

"Look, I like you, but you have issues. How many boys can you possibly like at a time?"

I hit Tyler in the arm, "Not that! I mean a little adventure to the Lewis' residence. We can make it there and back in good time."

"You might be able to, but I can't. Have you not seen my little chicken legs?"

He was right. He was having difficulty keeping up now, there was no way that he would survive the trek to Colton's house.

"If I sprint there, will you wait for me here? It's probably two miles there and back. I want to make sure Nate isn't there." I look at my watch, "Give me thirty minutes. If I'm not back, get out of here."

"Got it. I'll stay right here. Please be careful. Remember this, the code to the door is 1234, when you enter the library, go to the left and you will find a family portrait mounted to the wall. Cole pushes a nail to the right, located beside his head, and a panel will slide revealing a secret stairway. It leads directly to his bedroom."

"You are a true friend. I'll be back. How do you know their code?"

"Colton tells all of his friends."

I raced off sprinting through the tunnel. My only light was the beam from the flashlight. I started passing businesses. The bakery, the antique shop, the coffee shop, the post office, and then several homes. There were name plates on each door. This underground world has access to everything beneath the city. From the Lost World Cavern, to the north end of town at Persinger Farm, and up Route 60 including the businesses and homes. If the walls could talk, the stories that would be told.

Up the incline to the top of the hill, I recognize the name plate on the door as L-E-W-I-S, this must be the place. Gently I pry open the large wooden door and enter the code. There is an audible click and I realize that I have access of entry. Peeping through the door, there is silence. No one must be home. Concentrating on every step I take, I move to the portrait and then secretly up the stairs to Cole's room. Tidy and precise, everything is in place. No sign of anyone. I prowl around the edges of the room to ensure that there is no visible evidence of an intruder. As I complete my search, I recognize a picture frame protruding from underneath his bed. I lift it out for a closer inspection.

The picture from my mother's shop! I remember it from the hallway. There is a business man dressed in a grey suit, his wife, I presume, wearing a light blue party dress, and a dark haired girl, pretty in pink, sitting in front. The photo is taken inside the coffee shop, all three posed by the counter, with the name "Forde Café" printed neatly on the wall behind them. This is Sarah and her family. In a state of dismay, I remember the photo from the bathroom. The girl in the photo, the ripped in half photo, that created my locket, it was a picture of Cole and Sarah. The stunning, beautiful brunette is Sarah. I dash into the bathroom to find it, but the frame is empty. My whole world is flipped upside down. Why would Cole have the picture from the coffee shop of Sarah and her family?

I hear a car approaching from the main road and realize that I have to get out of here. My pulse races as adrenaline courses through my veins. Heart throbbing uncontrollably within my chest, perspiration droplets form on my forehead, I squeeze through the doorway entering the tunnel completing a flawless investigation. Dashing down the maze, jumping rocks, arms pumping cheek to cheek, and muscles in flight.

"You had three minutes, girl." Tyler shouted.

"Whew. That was exhilarating." I huffed as I catch my breath.

"What's in your hand?" Tyler pointed.

I look down and notice that I am still in possession of the frame. Taken by surprise, I forgot to put the picture back under the bed. Hopefully, Cole will not notice.

"That is a picture from underneath his bed."

"You stole a picture! Good Lord, Rachel. Have you lost your mind?"

"I didn't mean to. I heard someone and took off running." I replied, "it was under his bed, he won't miss it anyway." At least, I hope not.

"That is a picture of," Tyler paused as if paying respects to the family, "the Forde's. It was in Cole's room? That's odd."

"I don't get it. None of this makes sense."

Loud clambering, jingling, struggling can be heard from the upper end. Terrified that Cole knows someone was in his room, Tyler and I run away. After many, many steps, we stop to ensure that we are not being followed. It's clear.

"Nate isn't here, Tyler, let's get home." I implied.

"I'm with you. This is too much excitement for a pretty boy like me. I don't do well with confrontation."

"I got your back, Tyler."

"Rachel, I'm leaving," my mother called from her room, "Can you get up and watch your sister now?"

Oh, my head is pounding. All of that excitement last night, has given me a headache. I remember that there is no school today. A teacher ISE day, but for me, a sister PIA day.

"Rachel, come on. I need to leave." Lyn shouted.

"I'm up! I'll be in there in a minute." I yelled.

"Liar!" the little PIA replies. "Mom, she will stay in there all morning and starve me to death!"

"Bekah, you won't starve," I hear mom open the cabinet door, "here, start on Captain Crunch."

"Oh please." Bekah says as she rolls her eyes.

Climbing out of bed and fumbling to button my clothes, I start down the hallway. "I'm right here. Have a good day, mom. We are under control."

"Don't forget to charge your cell phone, Rae. I'll call later to see what you guys want for dinner."

My cell phone. I haven't seen it since last night. It wasn't on the charger. I remember holding it when I was with Tyler in the tunnel. I must have dropped it on the ground when I was leaving.

"Bekah, eat fast. We have to go for a ride."

"To McDonalds?" she asked.

"No. You have food."

"This sucks. I want pancakes, sausage, and a sweet tea." she demanded.

"Fine, you get ready and we'll stop by to get your food. Hurry." I begged.

Throwing on her Hello Kitty jacket, leopard boots, and hot pink scarf, Princess Bekah graces the world with her presence. For such a small human, she demanded the attention of everyone around her. Down the twisted road, fog covering the earth's surface, I think of the intelligent people counting sheep in their soft, warm beds. Not us, we are off to find a cell phone in a big field.

"This is not the way to Mickey D's, idiot." Bekah remarked.

"Really, genius." I rebutted, "I need to see if my cell phone is out here."

"In the woods. What were you doing in the woods? Smoochy, smoochy? Oh, Cole, I love you and your car."

"No, not in the woods. I was here with one of my girlfriends."

"Smooching?"

"No! We were looking for someone." I shake my head.

We cross the road into the field by the homeplace. I jump from my car to begin looking for my phone. Investigating under every strand of grass and under each fallen leaf. Bekah wanders around trying to actively participate in the search, in her own special way. She gazes into the sky admiring the clouds, probably trying to create visions of animals in her head.

"So, who's your friend?" Bekah asks.

"Okay, I won't lie to you. I was here with a guy friend looking for someone. No big deal."

"Ok, so who's your friend?" Bekah insists.

"His name is Tyler." I look at her bewildered and puzzled as to why she is so determined to know his name.

"No," Bekah loudly exhales, rolls her eyes, and places her hands on her hips, "that girl there." She point toward the old farmhouse.

"What girl?" I said.

"Right there." Pointing to a definite spot, "Can you not see the pretty girl? Is that your friend?"

Either my sister was trying to play a terrifying joke on me or she was viewing an apparition because there is nothing human before us.

"Ok, I'll play along," I take a deep breath, "what color hair does my friend have?"

"Dark, almost black."

"Her eyes? What color?"

"Brown." she replied.

"She sounds beautiful, Bekah," I follow her lead, "but, she sounds too perfect to be a friend of mine." I smile acknowledging her efforts of humor. I turn briskly to continue my search for the missing phone.

"Sarah says that you aren't as funny as you think you are." Bekah advised.

My heart skipped a beat. I whirled around to face my little sister. Her eyes focused straight ahead as if she examining something directly in front of her.

"Did you say Sarah?" my voice cracked.

"Goodness gracious, Rachel! She's right there and we are getting tired of you acting stupid. She said you've been here several times." Bekah turns her head listening to her spiritual friend, "She says that you don't pick up on things too fast. I'd have to agree with her." Bekah chuckles and continues speaking to herself.

"Where's Nate?" I asked.

"How would I know, Rachel? I don't have ESP, you know?" Bekah retorted.

Rolling my eyes to the back of my head, I remain calm not to upset princess, "No, does Sarah know where Nate is?"

"Why are you asking me? She is standing right in front of you. Ask her yourself. Geez. You are so lame." Bekah comments.

I stand in silence briefly trying to feel her presence. I am able to feel a chilly sensation around my hands as if she is touching them.

"Sarah, where is Nate? I need to find him." I said. The wind blows fiercely against the golden hay. The trees sway as the branches crack and pop from resistance.

"Bekah, anything?" I look at my sister for a response.

"Are we going to McDonalds?"

"What is she doing?"

"It'll cost you."

"YES, I will take you to McDonalds, now what did she say?" I demanded.

"She said she wants a sweet tea too." Bekah laughs at herself. "She didn't say anything, Rachel. She just moved over there by the hole in the ground and now she's gone. She didn't look upset. She was smiling like one of those little angels in diapers that you see on TV.

"She was wearing a diaper?" I hesitated.

"Her smile. Her smile was like one of those angels.", puffing and grumbling at my response she says, "You never listen to me. Whatever."

"She went over here to this hole?" I inquired.

"Do you see any others?" Bekah shouted with sarcasm.

I peered down inside the ruins of the house. Nothing was different from last night. Tyler and I followed it completely to downtown. I wonder if Nate came here after we left?

"Let's go inside." I offered.

"Are you crazy? I'm not getting dirty." Bekah exclaimed as she sternly crossed her arms in defiance.

"We will not get dirty. Come on."

"Absolutely not," she continues, "besides Sarah said you wouldn't find what you are looking for here. I guess your lover Nate is somewhere else."

Ignoring her attempt to start an argument, I spend several more minutes scanning the ground until finally I gave up hope. Bekah is lost in her own little world again, picking weeds and rocks from the ground. I believe one day she will be an architect or possibly a horticulturist. Her rock collection at home far exceeds anything I have accumulating dust.

"Alright, I'm done here. Let's get you something to eat." I say as we head towards the car.

As we pass through town, I see Colton's car parked in front of my mother's shop. I've never known him to stop by for coffee so I feel that it is out of character even for him. I turn after the stoplight changes green and do my best to parallel park in the narrow spaces the city calls parking places. My back tire rubs against the concrete edge vibrating the dashboard.

"Great." I said, "I'll have to replace that one too."

"You know," Bekah began, "Sarah said you need to open your eyes."

"What?", I slammed my brakes, "When did she say that?"

"In the field, before she went in the hole. I don't know what she's talking about, do you?"

"No, I can't say that I do." Bewildered and feeling nauseous, "Bekah, can you do me a favor, when you see Sarah again, will you tell me?"

"Can you not see her yourself?" Bekah whispered.

"No, I can't." I looked at my sister's angelic face as she tried to comprehend what I was telling her.

"Is she a ghost?"

Hesitantly I respond, "Yeah, I believe she is. I can hear her sometimes, but I can't see her.", I look at Bekah's trembling hands, "She won't hurt you. She's like a guardian angel or something. She was with me the day I fell and went to the hospital. Remember?"

"Yeah, I remember." she agrees.

"This is our little secret, Bekah. We can't tell anyone, not even mom. She'll think we're crazy."

"Or superheroes like those people on Fantastic Four." She grins with thoughts of having mysterious powers.

"Something like that." I smiled. "Let's visit mom so we can make plans for tonight. Can't find the phone, so we better check in."

Finding our way through the tables situated neatly within the shop, I see my mom and Cole sitting at one of the back tables. Laughing and smiling, they both look at us like we are uninvited guests intruding on a private conversation.

"Hey, mom. Bekah and I just stopped by to see how it was going today?" I interjected.

"Well, isn't this bizarre. You two are actually getting along?", mom looked surprised as I stood beside my little sister with my hand on her shoulder, "Colton came in to visit before he left town to see his grandmother."

"Oh, you're leaving town today?" I asked.

"Yes. I needed to make sure that you had all of my assignments before I left and since I tried to call you and didn't get an answer, I thought I would just leave them here with your mother. I hope that's alright with you."

"Of course. I can't find my phone right now. Who knows what I've done with it."

"Colton, Rachel loses things all the time. Phones, ipods, her Invisaligns, you name it, she's lost it." Lyn added.

"She's lost her mind too." Bekah added. I quickly nudged princess to remind her of our agreement. "Ouch." she grimaced.

"You'll find everything you need in the package, Rachel. I appreciate you taking care of that for me. I'll call you when I come back into town, okay?"

"Call the house. I'm not sure if I'll find my phone by then." I answered.

Colton softly smiled and said, “I’m sure you will find it by then. Just keep looking.” He turns to my mother, “Thank you for the fabulous conversation, Ms. Collins, I can see that Rachel has inherited your inner beauty.” He raises her hand and kisses it sweetly. Mom blushes. He turns to me wrapping his masculine arms around my shoulders, leans in to my ear and whispers, “I hope you found what you were looking for.” Kisses my forehead and saunters out the door.

My heart stops.

"Mom, I need to run a few errands. Can I see if Bekah can go to Natalie's for a little while?"

"Of course, is something wrong? You look as white as a ghost." Hearing my mother say those words, sent a cold chill up my spine.

"Everything is fine. I just have to do some things before school tomorrow and just remembered." I desperately search my pocket for the car keys, "I shouldn't be gone long."

"Why don't you go ahead. I can take her to Natalie's or she can hang out here with me. I shouldn't be late this evening; it's a slow day." mom said.

"Thanks, mom. I love you." I kiss mom on the cheek and turn to Bekah, "I love you too, kid." she smiles.

I grab Cole's package from the table and scurry out the door. My mind is racing. His words echo in my head. How did he know that I was looking for something last night? Did he follow us into the cave? Lindsey. I bet Lindsey told him about my excursion with Tyler. I decide to go to her house to confront her. She is supposed to be my friend, but all she has done is create drama. Maybe that is why Sarah says to open my eyes. People that I believe are my friends are only using me. For what, I have no clue. I have nothing to offer anyone.

Quickly, I pull out in front of oncoming traffic and speed through town. As I ascend the hill towards the Morgan's I notice Cole's car parked in front of his house. Do I ask him what he was talking about or do I go the source of the evil? Panicking and broken hearted, I whip the car into the driveway, missing the gate by inches. I hit the brakes abruptly giving warning that I have arrived with the loud squelch resounding from beneath my car. The creaking door shakes as I push it shut firmly and items rattle from the inside pocket. Up to the front door I sprint, heart pounding, words jumbled in my mind. The door bell rings.

No one responds.

I press the button again.

Still nothing.

As I reach down to touch the handle, the door eases open. I have been invited into the home. I step across the threshold not knowing what to expect. Silence.

"Colton?" I quietly call out. "Cole, are you here?" Silence. I decide that I will go upstairs to his room to see if he is there. To be honest, that's one of the only places I can find in this mansion. I see the library off to my left, but decide to take the normal route by using the stairs. The stairs that welcomed guests use.

"Colton?" again I call out, "Cole?" I hear a rustling noise coming from behind his door. Intoxicated by fear, my hand quivers as I reach to knock on his door.

"The door is open." I hear from the other side. It's him.

Entering the room, I see Cole sitting in the far corner, with his back faced towards me. The room is filled with darkness. The curtains are pulled shut and the lights are off. There is only a flickering light before him.

"So, this is the candle that you and Nate used the other night?" Cole probed.

I step towards him, "Nothing happened."

He turns to look at me in dismay. He knows that I have not been truthful with him.

"Tell me something, Rachel, when you were in the tunnel, did you find what you were looking for?" Cole responded.

"I went looking for answers about Sarah. No, I didn't find anything."

"Maybe you are searching in the wrong places." Cole glared at me. "Or maybe if you are with the wrong person, the answers will not be revealed."

"I am so sorry, Cole. It was a mistake. I just thought . . ."

"You just thought what? That Nate was innocent in all of this and that he would lead you to discover the truth. Open your eyes, Rachel!" Colton blurted.

I'm really starting to get annoyed with everyone telling me to do things that apparently I have no control over. I am oblivious to the world around me.

"Cole, I'm trying to see things for what they really are. Please understand that." I pleaded.

"You're not trying hard enough." He stands and starts towards me, "Let's go for a walk." He leads me to the secret door leading to the staircase. I pause briefly. "What's wrong?" he asks.

"Where are we going?"

"Just follow me. You've been there before." Cole grabs my hand and continues through the door leading from the library. We have entered the tunnel.

"Where are we going, Cole?"

"You want to look for answers, let's go find some answers. We will continue looking until you are satisfied." he demanded.

"Please don't be upset with me. I'm trying to understand what connection I have with Sarah, that's all."

Colton stops to face me. "Rachel, I want nothing more than for you to find yourself, to find peace within yourself, so I will do whatever it takes to put this behind us. I love you, Rachel Collins, do you hear me? I love you." Cole placed both of his hands on the sides of my face and kissed me. It is the most beautiful moment of my life. My heart skips a beat.

"I love you, too." For the first time, I realize that he does want the best for me. Nothing else matters. "We don't need to go any further, let's go back. It doesn't matter anymore. I'm happy with not knowing."

"No, Sunshine." Cole starts walking further, "Let's go one more time. Maybe you missed something before." He holds my hand tightly, gently squeezing occasionally to remind me that he cares.

We walk, and walk, and walk. It was so much easier when I sprinted the distance. It seems as if it is taking forever to reach the end. I look to the ground and notice that there are no footprints present as there were the other evening. Even with the gravel and clay, there are no visible signs of invasion.

"There's the shop entrances." I comment, "nobody coming out to play?" I snickered.

"I guess not. Maybe they only needed a picture." Cole replied as he picks up our pace.

"What did you say?" I questioned.

"A picture. Didn't your mother say that one of her pictures were missing?"

"Yeah," I murmured, "you're right." We continue along the corridor quietly.

Eventually, we reach the fork in the road. Straight ahead will lead us towards the courthouse and eventually the cavern. Nate would say go that way. To our right, we would end up at the farm. The decision of the road I've traveled several times or the road that leads to my memories with Nate.

"I say straight ahead." Cole replies, "We didn't go this way before. Let's see what we can find." Great. Memories with Nate it is, I think to myself.

The stream current sounds so peaceful flowing alongside us. The water trickling over rocks forming marsh-like, sodden reservoirs. Dampness occupies the surroundings creating a natural habitat for the underground ecosystem. I stoop to admire a miniature waterfall spewing between two large boulders whisking puny snails from fixation.

"Did you find something?" Cole jeered.

"No," I said deep in thought, "I was just thinking that sometimes I feel like these little guys," somberly I continue, "They are content to be where they are in life and then suddenly they are torn away from everything. Confused." I look at him, "I'm happy, Cole, but right now I am struggling. Why am I here, right now, in this place? Is it to find answers about your sister or is it to find answers about myself?"

"Well, maybe it's a little of both." He smiled while touching my shoulder and gently brushing through my hair, "Come on, let's see what we can find."

A heaviness comes over me, pressure within my chest, my breathing becomes labored as I gasp for air. The look of despair revealed in my eyes evident to my companion.

"Rachel, are you okay?" Cole says shockingly.

"Something is not right, Cole," I gasp, "Something is not right. Let me rest a moment." As I look over his shoulder, there she is . . . Sarah. A vision of beauty. Long, expresso brown hair, sweeping beneath her shoulders. Her almond shaped brown eyes glisten against her porcelain skin. I am so captivated by her pureness; her innocence.

"What's wrong?" Cole turns to witness my friend. "What are you looking at, Rachel?" he demands.

"Do you not see her?" I ask flustered.

"Her? No, all I see are rock walls and dirt." He turns towards me, "Who are you looking at, Rachel?"

"I believe it's Sarah." I said calmly.

He clutched my shoulders forcefully and thrust my body against the rigid wall. I could not overpower him as he struggled to grasp my wrists placing my arms behind my back.

"What are you doing?" I screamed.

"I've heard enough of this about Sarah", Cole cried out. "Sarah is dead. There is no Sarah!" He pressed my cheek against the chilled wall and whispered, "Where is Sarah now?"

Gone.

"How can you say that?" I pleaded.

Cole said nothing. Keeping his grip, he slowly moved us further into the tunnel. Relentlessly, I attempt to break free from his hold, but I have become his captive. Our feet shuffle through the dirt and gravel as we approach the location of my overnight stay with Nate.

"I know what you're doing. Your little friend, Brandon or maybe Tyler, told you where we were the other night," I said sarcastically, "I get it. You want to bring me down here so that I will feel guilty for being with him." I could feel the anger building inside me as my face flushed and hands trembled. "It's not going to work, Colton Lewis. I don't feel guilty. Nothing happened."

Cole stopped in his tracks and whirled me around to face him. "Nothing happened?" he smirked. "Nothing happened!" a cynical smile engulfed his face. "That's not what he said."

"Who Brandon or Tyler? Which one of your narks lied to you?" I yelled.

Cole shoved me again in the direction of our resting spot. In the distance, I could see a light coming from the chamber. As I looked to the ground, I could see fresh sets of footprints. The dirt reveals signs of an intense struggle. There are what appears to be three sets, it's hard to comprehend with all the impressionable scuff marks left as evidence.

"Why are you doing this, Cole? What are you trying to prove?" I begged.

"I want you to hear the truth."

We turn the corner to enter the chamber and I become paralyzed by the display before me. In a wooden chair, facing the farthest right corner, someone is sitting quietly. The only light evident in the room is a small candle that has been placed alongside the opposite wall. I strain my eyes to try to speculate who could be joining us for the evening but there has been a large sheet placed over their head to hinder my attempts of identification. I begin to writhe my hands in an attempt to break free. His grip tightens as he leads me to the prisoner and shoves me at their feet. I hit the floor and scoot against the wall not knowing who is under the concealment.

"Rachel wants the truth." Cole begins, "Rachel doesn't trust me and she wants the truth." I can see him glaring from the corner of my eyes, but I have not veered from his captive. "Well, Sunshine, I will let you here it from the source." Cole strolls to the chair, holds one corner of the cloth in his hand and with one quick tug, he tears away the covering.

“Nate?” I cried. There sat my hero with a black eye and dried blood streaming from his nose. Behind his back, his wrists have been tied and around his mouth was a tightly bond gag so that he could not speak although his eyes told me everything. He was terrified. I crawled to his chair to loosen his restraints, but was hastily knocked into the wall.

“No, no, no Sunshine. Nate will be able to leave when he explains everything to you.” Colton paced in front of the chair, “He will be able to leave when he admits to everything that he has done.” He stops in front of the chair, “Don’t worry, the others will be here soon. I’ve called a little meeting.”

“Others? What are you talking about?” I turn to face the captive, “Nate, are you okay?” he shuts his eyes and slowly nods his head in affirmation.

“If the truth needs to be told, then everyone involved needs to be present.” Cole folds his arms and contemplates his next move.

“Just let us go. I don’t care anymore. Just let us go.” I plead.

“No, Rachel. I love you and I won’t let you go. You need to open those pretty, little eyes of yours and understand that what you see around you, this is reality. You have choices to make in life and you need to think of everyone involved, not just yourself.”

“Who is involved? You, Nate, and me. Got it.”, I blurted, “now, let’s all go home and pretend that this never happened.

Without saying a word, Cole walks to his captive and removes the cloth from his mouth.

“Rachel, I am so sorry.” Nate whispers.

“What, Nate, you are so sorry? For what?” Cole kicks his chair, “for falling in love with my girl? Did you not learn a lesson the last time?” he exclaims.

I shake my head from side to side as my eyes turn to Nate. His eyes filling with tears, begin to stream down his face. Broken and degraded, he can not even look me in the eyes.

"Last time? What is he talking about Nate?" I asked.

Slowly glancing up from a stupor, Nate whispers, "Sarah". With hearing this, my heart quivers in an arrhythmic fashion.

I pivot to face Colton, "I thought Sarah was your adopted sister?"

"She was", he paused, "after her parents untimely passing."

"Untimely, my ass! Your family set that up so that your father could have sole ownership of the company!" Nate growls.

Cole shakes his head as if scolding a child and makes a "tisk, tisk, tisk" sound as he does so. "Nate, do you honestly believe that we could get away with something like that?"

"Your family owns every lawyer, police officer, and judge in town. Yeah, I do."

"Ok, so maybe we do, but why did Sarah come to live with us, Nate?" Cole jeered.

"Because you controlled her mind, much like you are doing to Rachel." Nate pleads with me, "Rachel, you have to see through his deception."

"No, she came to live at our house because she loved ME." Cole paces back and forth, "Not you, Nate, she loved me." He pauses in front of his chair, "and when she told you that, you were so angry that you killed her!"

"I would never do that, I loved her." Nate cried.

"You were that last to see her that night when you were fighting. You didn't come back to join us. You followed her." The accuser looks at me and back to Nate, "please tell me if I'm wrong."

Nate looks at the ground before him, "No, I followed her, but couldn't find her."

"At least that's your side of the story,but why don't we ask for her?", Cole stares blankly into the room, "Sarah, will you please tell us your side of the story?", a long silence, "Oh, that's right, she can't because she's dead!" Cole hits Nate's jaw so fiercely that his head whips as blood splatters on my shirt.

"Please, stop!" I beg.

"Oh, we're not done, yet." Cole, saunters to and fro, "So, why were you conveniently at the gas station the night of our little argument, Nate?"

"I was following her." he whispered.

"What?", Cole questioned, "I couldn't hear you?"

"I was following her." he said louder.

"Stalking is more like it there, buddy."

"I was there long enough to see Brandon flatten her tire. Does that help?" Nate chimed in.

Cole's eyes pierced through Nate. Again, he raced towards Nate as I threw myself in front of him. "Enough! Stop hitting him. If you want me to hear the truth, damn it, tell me! I'm so sick of these games!" I turned to Cole, "Tell me the truth, Cole! If you love me, tell me the truth!"

"You want the truth, Sunshine?" Colton said.

Suddenly, two more bodies emerge from around the corner. Brandon and Lindsey. Gasping for air and perspiring, I can see that they have exerted a lot of their energy.

"Man, I thought you were waiting for us?" Brandon asked.

"The party was started a little early. Our friend, Nate, was so forthcoming with his apologies that I couldn't control it any longer." Cole replied.

I glance at Lindsey as she gives me her signature look of displeasure. "Lindsey, you're in this too?"

She says nothing. Brandon places his arm around her shoulders and replies, "Our little Lindsey, she is a follower."

"Ok, Cole, the gang's all here. Let's hear it." I said.

"You don't get it, do you Rachel?" Cole glared at me as he turns to Nate.

Annoyed, I said, "What, the little Caving Club? Yeah, I get it, President Lewis."

Cole immediately pivots to face me, "Oh, Rachel," he shakes his head as he approaches, "this is so much more than a club," he continues, "years ago our families were bound together by circumstances that we will never fathom."

"Our families?" I questioned, "My family is not in the same social standing as yours."

"Maybe not now, but they were." Nate replied, "Look around you, Rachel, did you not read the walls?"

It all makes perfect sense now. The names on the walls: Lewis, McClung, Morgan, Johnson, Forde, and Collins. I don't understand the dates, but the names of their descendants are all standing with me in this room.

"So, you organized all of this? You are the puppet master?" I asked sarcastically.

"Puppet master? No, we are all together for a reason." Cole replies.

"Has your mother not told you about the coffee shop, Princess?" Brandon adds.

Looking at Brandon in dismay, "What about the shop?"

Colton steps forward to regain our attention, "All of our families own shops downtown. Shops that are linked by the tunnel system." He begins to pace in front of his audience, "Family secrets are buried with our ancestors that need to be revealed." Cole exclaimed

"You have no idea what you are talking about. My mother bought that shop when we moved here from Florida." I argued.

"Why would your family move to this little town from Florida? Well, Sunshine, that is because she inherited the shop from her family, the Johnson's." Cole walks to me, "You, my friend, have dual lineage. You do not realize how significant you are to our group." He pauses in front of me, "You must be protected."

Johnson? Johnson . . . it is true. My grandmother in Florida was a Johnson. "But I thought that the Forde's owned the coffee shop?"

"Yes, Rachel. The owners were John Forde and Deidre Johnson Forde. After their accident, the shop was transferred to the next heir, your mother. Of course, she would immediately return to her ancestors hometown." Cole said with a crooked grin.

"I didn't have anyone in my family by the name Deidre." I looked at everyone puzzled.

"Small town secrets. Let's just say, many people in this town share more than a casual conversation. It wasn't public knowledge, Rachel."

"Then Sarah had a dual lineage also. Why would she lead me into the tunnel?" I looked at Cole, "Why didn't I just get an official invite into your club like everyone else?"

"Sunshine, you must have had a hard bump on that noggin of yours," Cole sneers, "Let's go back to the beginning," he continues as Brandon snickers, "the house at Persinger Farm. That wasn't Sarah that you saw, that was Lindsey. She and I were, well, exploring and I must have upset her."

"You were exploring something alright." Brandon interrupts.

Cole glares at his friend as he continues, "As I was saying, she ran outside, saw you, and scurried back in. You followed for a while inside the tunnel until I had to knock you over the head with a rock and drag your body back out to the pit." Cole looked to Lindsey, "then Florence Nightingale over there, was afraid that you would die, so she looked at your phone to get your mother's number. To get back at me, she used the name Sarah knowing that she would get the attention that she so desires." Again, he paces in front of his spectators, "to see if you remembered anything, of course I made sure that I went on the emergency call with the squad. Soon I realized that you didn't remember anything so, I didn't worry." Cole walks to me, "then, you were just so cute that I couldn't resist the temptation."

"But inside the cave? She heard Sarah in the cave?" Nate said.

"That's where it gets bizarre. Rachel, you claim to see her. I don't believe you. I think the bump on your head has made you delirious."

I did not even respond.

"Then Nate gets involved. I'm not stupid. I can see that you were trying to sabotage the relationship." Cole laughs as he glares at his captive, "but she wanted me."

"Tristan and Kamryn in the graveyard? What was that?" I questioned.

"Planned." Colton gives Brandon a high five, "We were to follow them that night. I wanted you to see the underground tunnel. It's my home away from home." He smiles, "Then, they sneak out the door with the picture from your mother's wall."

"What is so special about the picture?" I questioned.

"Did you look at it closely the other night when you stole it from my house?" Cole stared through me.

"No, I didn't." I said matter of factly. "How did you know that I was there?"

"Oh, sorry," Cole reaches into his pocket and takes out my cell phone, "you must have dropped this when you ran from my room. That was close." He looks to Brandon, "we were almost busted dragging your sweet, precious Nate into the cave." He turns back to face me, "Now, the picture . . . what about the picture in the bathroom? Notice anything?"

"I saw you and I am presuming, Sarah, yes." I pointed out.

"Nate, do you know the answer?" Brandon quizzed.

"The necklace." he murmured.

"Yes, the necklace." Cole commended. "I didn't think that Nate would remember the necklace, but I guess he did." He squats in front of Nate, "I hated to see it go to waste, so I thought I would take it from one girlfriend to give to another."

Nate tries to stand from the chair but is still restrained from the backside. "You asshole!" Nate yelled. "You knew that I loved her." He sits back down realizing that he cannot escape.

"And see, Rachel, I knew that Nate would eventually tell you everything. That's why when he and Brandon were wrestling on the ground the other day, we took his phone. Perfect actually", he continues, "we sent you a text saying that you wouldn't see him again, you were the last to see him, the cops look at you as a suspect, it goes as planned. We kidnap him, unsuspectingly, and here he is."

"The note on the car? Brandon too?" I asked.

"Yes. That was his idea." Cole explained.

I look at Brandon, puzzled, "Well, Lindsey is not the only one that is a follower, now is she?" I smirk.

"You Bi . . ." Brandon starts to say.

"That's right." Lindsey says as she winks at me.

I am exhausted from the drama and ready to finish this conversation, "Ok, so now I know the whole story." I look to Brandon, "Brandon is your bitch, steals, flattens tires, has horrible handwriting, and fights like a girl," Lindsey laughs as I continue, "Lindsey goes along with whatever you all ask her to do because she loves you Cole", her eyes drop to the floor and there is silence, "Nate was madly in love with Sarah and Cole wasn't having any of that, literally," Brandon chuckles, "and Cole, you are just crazy. Crazy for loving your soon to be sister, crazy for killing her out of jealousy, and crazy for thinking that I would ever be with someone as ruthless and heartless as yourself."

"Tell us how you really feel, Rachel." Brandon cynically replies. "Where in the world did she come from? Is this our Rachel?"

"I still have one question, though." I walk to Cole, "Where is Sarah's body?"

"Gone." He looks at his peers, "She's dead and gone."

I cannot believe what my ears have just perceived. Colton Lewis has basically admitted that he has evidence of Sarah Forde's death.

"And how do you know that?" I asked. "Were you there when it happened? Did you become so angered by jealousy that you killed her and your little minions helped you move the body beneath Lewisburg? Did you drag her body through the tunnels so everyone would consider her a runaway?" I gracefully move towards Cole, "You didn't realize you placed her body too close to the stream and that it would rise with heavy rainstorms and flush her remains out at the drainage. Did you not think about burying her a little deeper? The ground was too solid from the hardened clay, wasn't it?" I stand before Cole, the murderer, and continue, "I will ask you again, Cole, how do you know that she is dead?"

Cole stares blankly at me and then to Nate. Silence fills the air and the only sound heard is the gurgling bubbles of the stream outside the chamber along with the trickling of water as it spews from the rocks. I have just provided him with details unknown to many. That must have been what happened that night of her disappearance. It seems so real to me.

"Because I saw," he paused

"What, Cole, what did you see?"I screamed.

Exhaling loudly, Cole continues," Because I saw you . . ."

The world begins to spin as my body becomes weak. I can feel my heart beating uncontrollably as my accuser stands before me with this horrid allegation. Memories of my family and friends reciprocate again and again in my mind. My body becomes numb and lifeless as if every ounce of my being has departed from my human form. I cannot breath, I gasp for air, choking as I try to speak. My eyes quickly become obscured from tears as I become overwhelmed with disbelief. Did I just recollect my part in this plot to kill Sarah. Could I have done this? The stream no longer audible, the soothing rush of water over pebbles and stones, now I go into nothingness . . . .

"We've got her back!", a man's voice demanded, "Kids, friends, you'll all need to join the others outside the room until she is stable. Won't be long, she came back strong. I've never seen someone fight this hard."

As I listen to the many voices in the space around me, they all seem familiar. I can hear my mother, Bekah, Cole, Nate, Lindsey, Brandon, Tyler, Louella, Wesley, Janella, Gerald, Carrington, Jake, Dylan, and Emily. It's a jumbled mess of words in varying tones and crying. My body shivers as I feel a sharp pain in my arm that is laying by my side. I can hear the rhythmic sound of the air as it flows through my lungs. The dripping of water is now replaced by a softened chirp that accompanies my heartbeat.

"Open your eyes, Sunshine. Listen to me, open your eyes." a male voice so endearing speaks. That must be my father.

"Rachel, I know that I've said this before, but I love you and I won't let you go. Open those pretty little eyes of yours." a mother's voice is unforgettable.

"Get your ass out of bed." Chuckling at himself, that would be my step father, enjoying his own humor.

"Is she dead?" and there is the little sister.

"She's not dead, honey, the doctor said that she had been in an accident. She'll be fine."

"What about the split in her head? Is her brain going to come out?" the innocent voice asked, "Will she remember me?"

How could I forget. That is my little sister, Rebekah. As I lay here and listen to my family, I realize that while I've been with my friends chasing ghosts, I was actually following my guardian angel who rescued me. Through caves, tunnels, fields and back, she protected me along the way. I never knew she had a name, but from this time forward, it will be Sarah.

"Will she be okay, mam?" I heard a knock at the door. I tried to peek through my eyelids to catch a glimpse of this particular voice. I fondly remember it so well.

"Yes, she will be fine. Thank you for taking such good care of her," mom paused briefly, "so you start medical school here soon?" I could sense her smiling, "How wonderful."

"Yes, mam. Well, when she wakes up, please give her this. I found it laying beside her. I tried to rub the mud off, but she will probably need to have it properly cleaned." There are footsteps, "I can't stay, I've got to get back to the others. I'll hopefully see you again soon." Again, footsteps followed by a shutting door.

"Oh, what a beautiful locket." I hear the clasp open abruptly, "No pictures inside though, that's odd." the locket shuts, "What a miracle that boy found her. If he wouldn't have seen her footprints, we would have never seen her alive." my mother explained.

I'm sure that there is a lesson to be learned through this adventure of ours and one day it will all be revealed. As for me, I will look for footprints everywhere I go. I can choose to follow the path well trodden or I can choose to create my own. Whichever way I go, I am certain that my Sarah will be there with me. I do hope that she is well prepared, because my story . . . it's just beginning.